There is no greater wish than for a prince who is brave, strong, and true...

CHAPTER 1

A young man stood on a scaffold waiting for death.

Guns and drums surrounded him. A priest read proverbs from a Bible, the spine cracked with age.

"Prince Philip, by proclamation of King Rupert, you have been condemned to death on this day, the sixth of May in the year of our Lord one thousand seven hundred and ninety-one. May God have mercy on your soul," a man announced to the crowd. He reeked of palace protocol.

The prince remained standing tall, not a quiver daring betray the fear bleeding through his eyes. Three guards made to remove his coat, but he put out his hand stopping them.

With a shake of his shoulders he slid his coat off himself. His fingers twisted within his cravat, unraveling the jungle of fabric from around his neck. He unbuttoned his shirt revealing his chest and peeled the collar away from his skin.

One of the guards grabbed his hair, yanking his head back causing him to stumble. Still he did not protest. Scissors gleamed in the sun as they ate through his tresses, leaving jagged tufts of hair in its wake. The guard threw his severed ponytail to the crowd, and a dozen hands rose into the air hoping to catch a souvenir.

It made my stomach churn.

"I never thought I'd see the day a prince be executed. Now I've seen twenty-seven!" an old woman said next to me. "Still they come, all wanting a taste of the power the king offers. Greed is what I call it."

Wire-like gray hair sprung out from beneath her moth eaten bonnet. What teeth remained in her mouth were a mixture of black and yellow. Her eyes shone with an odd mixture of childlike simplicity and severe reality.

"I think that harsh," I replied. "They are only doing what comes natural to the truly desperate."

"Truly stupid is more like it," she retorted. "Is power ever worth risking one's own life?"

"That depends on the reward." I pulled on the strap of my satchel.

I had not come for a chat. Leaning on my cane, I stepped away from her and neared the scaffold.

The prince put out his hands and they were quickly tied behind his back. Head held high, the guards escorted him to the railing. The jeers of the crowd died away in anticipation of his final royal address.

"I die having failed King Rupert. I die having failed your kingdom," he said, voice remaining firm. "I accept my judgment. I am no coward. I only pray another will be stronger than I and fulfill His Majesty's quest."

"Pull the lever already!" course men chanted between swigs of whiskey.

Four guards latched onto the prince's arms and tugged him back towards the guillotine. They pushed him down onto his stomach and locked stained wooden boards around his neck. The blade hung ready to plummet towards the feast of soft flesh below.

The crowd was in a frenzy, and a roar filled the square. They clapped their hands around their mouths and hooted and hollered to the executioner. They hungered for blood.

"Get on with it!" a woman holding a small child jeered.

A loud cry cut through the growl and drums began to rumble. The priest's prayers disappeared behind the tumbling succession of sticks against taught leather. The prince closed his eyes.

I had seen a hundred men do the same in war. Even the bravest could not face their death square on. For this, he had my pity.

"Pull it!" the crowd snarled.

A click and a rush rang out followed by splitting bone.

It was done.

Cheers erupted.

Blood rained down the wood and pooled in the crevices of the cobblestones. Elbows jabbed into stomachs as onlookers scurried towards the scaffold, white handkerchiefs in hand. They dabbled up whatever crimson they could as grim tokens and mementos. A prince's blood could fetch a pence or two, enough for a loaf of bread to slake their hunger.

Disgust filled me not at the death of a youth, but at what the king had made of his own people. Animals living in squalor. That would all change soon. I dove my hand into my satchel, grounding myself within the silken layers of the cloak that promised me the crown.

The prim man who had read the charges reached into the basket for their newest trophy. His fingers coiled within the prince's blonde hair as he held the head to the crowd. The eyes that minutes before showed fear were now vacant, the lips slack and skin flushed blue.

"King Rupert requires a new challenger," he said. "One who is cunning enough to solve the mystery baffling His Majesty. Any man may accept this quest as long as they are resolute. As a reward, they will inherit King Rupert's throne. But," he held up the prince's head even higher, "if the contender is unable to solve the mystery in three days, he will face the same fate as our freshly departed Prince Philip."

I cleared my throat to rid the dry prickle that seized it and pulled again on the strap of my satchel. The reassuring heaviness vanquished the trepidation he tried to instill. This was the moment I traveled so far for, and I would not abandon my fellow citizens as had our king.

"I will be your new challenger!" I called out.

An ocean of eyes locked on me. Several onlookers crossed their chests that were stained with dirt and muck.

I approached the scaffold, planting my cane firmly into the cobblestones. Pain split through my ankle with each step, but I ignored it as always.

"Tosser!" Someone yelled.

The man's face pinched into a sharp point and his eyes flashed with irritated doubt. It was a look I was all too familiar with. It was a look I was wearisome of seeing.

"It is illegal to mock the crown," he warned.

Guards brought him the basket and he swiftly dropped Prince Philip's head inside as if it were nothing more than a banana peel.

"I do not mock." I stood right below him now. "I want to be His Majesty's next challenger."

Laughter bubbled out of the throats of the crowd causing my every muscle to tighten.

"Sir, you are..." he took in a breath, "*lame*."

"I am well aware. Does that exclude me?"

He blinked several times as if thinking what to reply.

"No, I suppose it doesn't."

He wiped the smattering of blood on his hand away with his kerchief and flew down the creaking stairs.

"I'm Lord Charles Langley," he said, holding out his hand. "And you are?"

My lip curled in revulsion seeing red still smeared across his signet ring.

"Ross Daltry," I replied.

Awkwardness filled the space between us as I continued to let his arm hover. He stretched it further towards me until he saw I would not be swayed. I had little use for etiquette anymore.

"Mr. Daltry, if you are quite determined..."

"I am," I said, growing impatient. "Is there a document I sign? Or do I make a pledge? I wish to be in His Majesty's services immediately."

The man seemed dumbfounded for a second or two, as if thinking my mind would still change. He could never guess the determination rushing through my every vein.

"A meeting with the king is usually all that is required, Mr. Daltry. I will inform His Majesty of your intentions to become his—" he paused at the word, "—champion."

"Is that all?" I inquired further.

He sighed.

"Arrive this evening at the palace gates. State your name to the guards. Everything will follow suit from there," he said. Then, he hesitated. "I...suggest you take these remaining hours and think through what you are doing. I do not want the king's time wasted on a rash moment of bravery. Men half your age and...vigor...have met the blade."

I glared at him wanting to put him beneath the blade.

"I do not waste time," I said. "Not my own, and especially not the king's."

CHAPTER 2

Though May, a chill still clung to the air and blew easily through the holes in my wool jacket. I tugged on the fraying fabric and closed it as best I could, walking carefully across the cobblestones that spread before the palace gates.

Through the iron bars an immense structure of shades of yellow rose up from the earth. Large panes of glass reflected the bits of sun peeking through the clouds.

I gripped the cold iron and peered at the grounds where the king and his band of nobles resided. A far cry from the damp forests and putrid barns I was forced to live in as a parasite thanks to them. My grasp tightened on the bars.

It is your destiny to discover the secret King Rupert seeks. Remain brave, strong, and true, and all will unravel as it should.

White eyes flashed like splitting lightning as the Oracle's words floated through my memory. There was no reason to doubt her prophesy. Desperation doesn't allow reason. She handed me the cloak that now resided in my satchel and I accepted the fate she told me was mine to take.

"Get away. Don't want the likes of you," A guard barked,

breaking my memory. Red spots speckled his skin, his demeanor one of rash youth.

"Get!" a second shouted, this one larger and older. Murder filled his green eyes as he pointed his bayonet at my chest.

It would take more than two goons to frighten me.

"I am here at the request of Lord Charles Langley," I said. "I'm here to serve His Majesty the king."

Their red uniforms jingled with their rolls of laughter.

"You look more ready to scrub out the palace's chamber pots then have an audience with His Majesty," the large one jested. "I can barely make out your face through that dense stubble."

"He don't look that bad," the other replied. "He still has most of his buttons on that old suit. He'd be better suited braiding the horses' tails."

I gripped my cane, fighting the urge to bash them both over the head.

"My name is Ross Daltry," I hissed. "Now, you can tell Lord Charles Langley I am here, or I will continue on through those gates and you can damn well shoot me. When the king discovers you killed his next challenger, I am sure he will be most understanding."

Their jeering smiles flattened into grimaces.

"Perkins, fetch Lord Langley," the older one said, jabbing his elbow into the ribs of the younger. "This gent can be his problem. I'm growing bored of him."

Perkins sniffed as if disappointed the fun was over, but turned and did as he was commanded.

I did not wait long.

Lord Langley hurried across the cobblestones. The gold buttons of his maroon suit shimmered against his cream vest and for three seconds jealousy flushed over me. A lead ball saw to it I would never again wear the finery of my youth, and all the king's medals meant nothing with a crushed ankle.

"Mr. Daltry!" he exclaimed, rubbing his soft hands together. "I was curious if you'd come or not. Still not dissuaded, I see."

His eyes fell again to my cane, and disapproval pulled at his lips.

"Should I be?" I asked in a flat tone.

His gaze jumped back up to meet my own, and he laughed awkwardly.

"Of course not! Please, do follow me," he said with false graciousness.

He turned on his black heels and took off towards the palace doors. I lifted my cane and stabbed the ground hard with each step as I shuffled behind him. He looked back over his shoulder at me, checking on me as if I were a child.

"Do I need to walk slower?"

"I can walk whatever pace is required of me."

Marble and stone soon encased us as we entered the palace doors. I limped across the black and white tiles that stretched down every hall. My ankle strained and burned with every step. With each wince or shudder I blocked the pain by keeping my gaze squarely on the man in front of me.

If it was a pulsing sting I focused on the space between his shoulders where his jacket wrinkled. If it was a raw flash, I counted the curls of his wig.

"Not much farther," he said.

We walked through three more halls passing candelabras, portraits, and windows that stretched from floor to ceiling. Exquisite finery the king's people could never fathom. Thankfully our journey ended when we encountered a closed door of inlaid wood.

After straightening his jacket and smoothing his wig he turned the sculpted handle and pulled the door open. I found myself staring at a tall man surrounded by white paint and golden motifs.

His gaze remained on the leather bound book he was reading behind a polished wooden desk. He was all angles and muscle, though gray feathered through his blonde hair. His blue sash and red heeled shoes made it clear who he was.

"Your Majesty," Lord Langley said. "May I present Mr. Ross Daltry. Your new champion."

King Rupert snapped his book shut and tossed it on the desk beside a stack of papers. He leaned back in his damask chair and looked at me. His blue eyes hinted at severity, though his smile put me immediately at ease.

"I am pleased you haven't let Langley scare you off," he said. "When you are offering a reward such as mine, you need to make sure only the most serious apply."

"Everything I do is with serious consideration, Your Majesty," I replied.

His smile widened at this and he gave an appreciative nod.

"Langley, leave us," he said, his eyes not leaving mine.

Lord Langley tensed as if wanting to say something further, but bowed, leaving me alone with the king and two servants.

King Rupert dug his fingers into a silver bowl of walnuts and rummaged through.

"I have sent twenty-seven princes to the guillotine," he said. A nutcracker appeared in his right hand. "Those are only the ones that have returned. Dozens more have simply gone missing. The cowards. Afraid of their fate, the lot of them. If I ever hear a whiff of where they've run off, I will track them down and slit their throats myself." The walnut cracked and split in one swift movement. He retrieved the nut from the fragments of shell and popped it in his mouth. "My hands drip with blood, Mr. Daltry. Now you wish to redden them further."

"Does Your Majesty already have so little faith in me?" I asked.

He didn't answer. Rising from his chair he approached me, the floorboards creaking beneath him. He circled once around me, his gaze boring into mine as if demanding my faults rise to the surface.

I wanted to ask him if I should whinny like one of his prized race horses. It would not have been a far stretch. Nobility always believed breeding determined greatness.

"You are far older than the other applicants," he said. "They have all been strapping young men. Learned in battle and in classics."

I did my best to hold back a smile. "Yet all have failed Your Majesty."

He chuckled darkly. "I suppose Chaucer can only offer so much protection," he remarked. "But youth does have its benefits. Pray, what is your age?"

"Forty-three, Sire," I replied.

He thought a moment, running his finger over his lips.

"I suppose years are only added wisdom," he said. "Perhaps it is time for some heartier stock. You have a strong build and pockmarks do not ravage your skin as most of your station. Your constitution must be excellent."

How decent of him to notice.

"My years in Your Majesty's army made me so, Sire."

His right eyebrow rose.

"Where did you serve?"

"I fought at the Battle of Dunlap," I replied. "I was decorated with the Golden Spur for Acts of Bravery."

The king's face brightened and he slapped me on the shoulder.

"Good lad!" he said. "That battle is the only reason I am still king. Twelve-hundred of my soldiers against an army of two thousand. I don't have to tell you how many men we lost that day. How many strong horses! The kingdom's wealth was two days away from being completely empty. Even the palace had to ration food as the people. We all had to make sacrifices for the crown."

I wanted to laugh thinking of his great sacrifice of eating trout instead of lamb. His eyes fell down to my cane.

"It appears your sacrifice was greater than most," he said.

I straightened my posture best I could to prove my capabilities. "I assure you Sire, my injury will not dampen my ability to solve the riddle that vexes you."

"I don't doubt it!" he said. "In fact, that injury only says one thing to me. You aren't afraid to face death for your king. I need such bravery now more than ever."

"I will do whatever is required. I always have."

This seemed to please him as he waved me to follow him.

"Let me show you what vexes me," he said.

He removed a small brass key from his breeches as we neared a door at the opposite end of the room. A small click and it opened wide revealing a sight I never knew possible.

Shoes.

Mountains of tattered shoes filled a cavernous room up to the arched ceiling. Blue. Pink. Yellow. Satin and silk tore at every seam. Purple. Gold. Red. Worn soles popped away from fraying fabric. Silver. Black. Green. Heels cracked down the middle. Toes split through silk. Ribbons were edged with fraying threads.

"Every night my twelve daughters are locked in their room. There is no way in or out. Yet, every night, their shoes are left nothing but mangled rags," he said. "It is beyond all comprehension."

I walked in and picked up an orange slipper. Ribbons unraveled down my fingers, and the sole peeled away from the cloth and fell to the floor. Anger burned in my heart seeing such waste to the point of making me ill. A single pair would have fed an entire family for three days.

I swallowed down my own hunger.

"Can you not stop paying for them?" I asked.

King Rupert stiffened, and blotches of red blossomed across his face.

"I don't pay for them at all!" he exclaimed. "Do you really think I'd permit such foolishness?"

I was the wrong person to ask. To me, he had always been foolish.

"Then how do they fund them? If there is one thing I know it's that money does not sprout like daisies."

"This is part of the mystery you are to solve. The princesses have an allowance, yet every month it is never exceeded," he said. "I run my kingdom in order and this defies that order. I refuse to let it stand a moment longer."

The answer to this quandary seemed a simple one. Thieves. That is what his daughters were. The finery they had already been blessed with was not enough to satiate their greed.

I wondered who they bribed and with what favors to keep such a secret from their own father. They rejoiced in their materialism while their own people were happy to afford a loaf of yesterday's bread.

"What does Your Majesty wish I do?"

"End it," he said. "Discover what they do at night and how their shoes become destroyed. I offer you my entire kingdom to know their secret. You can marry the daughter of your choosing. At my death, you will be king."

I threw the tattered shoe back on the pile. Several others toppled down and fell to pieces on the floor.

"Gladly," I said.

"You will have three days and three nights. Time is of the most importance. If you do not succeed...well, you know the consequence," he said, his expression darkening.

"I have no fear," I said.

He cocked his head and looked at me as if I were an odd wonder.

"You are the oldest by far, not to mention also lame, yet you do not shirk as so many others have done. Why take on such a challenge?" he asked.

I paused.

I wanted the crown to rule the people as they deserved to be ruled. For once in their miserable lives they would know justice. Equality. Not have their last pennies snatched for taxes to pay for the crown's feasts and parties. Nobility had forgotten us, but soon they would hear us roar.

I could hardly tell him this truth.

"I am a natural born soldier," I said, instead. "My instinct is to serve my country...and my king."

I tried to not make this last word hard or hint at my disgust. His chest puffed out as if truly believing my false flattery. He motioned me back to his room and closed the door. Turning to one of the servants he nodded and the man left.

"You are definitely not a prince, but we cannot afford to be picky," he said.

The tapping of heeled shoes and shifting of fabric echoed down the hall. The servant returned and held the door open as a throng of young women walked in.

Tight curls sprung out around pretty faces before cascading past their slender shoulders. Silk sashes tied around their waists and lace fichu's puffed over their bosoms. They were all swathed in soft creams and pale purples and pinks except for one who was dressed in striking stripes of green.

They lined up before their father and gave a deep curtsy.

"My daughters," King Rupert said looking upon them with fatherly pride. "The youngest Aloysia, then we have Caroline, Dorothea, Charlotte, Camilla, Aurelia, Henrietta, Sophia, Amelia, Matilda, and the eldest, Octavia."

Octavia curtsied deeply, her striped gown billowing

around her. There was an air of charge in her manner, from the delicate way she held out her skirts to the elegant stiffness of her back and neck. Her skin had never seen the sun and her cheeks were flushed with rouge. Her blue eyes rose to meet my gaze and her plump, pink lips spread into a smile.

For two seconds I wanted to feel her lips against my own.

Was I seriously already going mad over a pair of fine eyes? I blamed my tight cravat and cursed myself inwardly for being foolish. I had no time to be distracted by women, especially selfish ones.

"This is Mr. Daltry," King Rupert said. "He has taken my challenge and will be our new champion."

"Pleasure to meet you, Mr. Daltry," their melodious voices said in unison.

"I trust you will treat him with the utmost respect," their father added. "Until he proves otherwise, he is the next heir to the throne."

His face beamed turning to me. I tugged on the strap of my satchel, the Oracle's prophesy not far from my thoughts.

"Yes, Sire," they sang.

"Then it is settled," the king said. "All that is left is for you to take an oath."

He pulled out a small Bible from his breast pocket. I withheld a chuckle and my scorn.

"Place your right hand over the word of God," he directed.

I did as he commanded, pressing my fingers against the stiff leather. I wondered how much he had followed the scripture inside. The perfect pages told me the binding had never once been cracked.

"Swear to your king and your God, that you will do all you can to solve the mystery I seek. That you will risk your life for your king, and give your life for your king should you fail," he said.

My chest constricted, and my words stuck in my throat. I had to subjugate myself to the two entities I despised. I breathed deeply, realizing I was a man with little choice if I wished to push forward.

"You have my word, King Rupert," I said, grinding out the words, every syllable chaining myself to God and king.

Secretly, in the depths of my soul, I spoke the words to the people and myself.

You have my word.

In that moment, I would not fail. I could not.

CHAPTER 3

I was expected for dinner.

The valet grumbled about the state of my torn jacket, though I wasn't sure if it was the missing buttons and ripped seams that bothered him more or the fact it was a decade behind fashion. Peeling it off my shoulders with glee he tossed it aside and barked at a servant to fetch me something sleek and modern.

I quickly found myself sat in a chair with a razor scraping across my chin and cheeks. My rumpled brown hair was combed and tied with a black satin ribbon. The servant returned with a blue suit causing a cascade of approving French to fall from the valet's mouth.

It was gratifying as silk kissed my skin once again, though the sleeves were tighter and the collar higher. Standing before a full length mirror I saw a man I had not seen in twenty years.

His face was more angles than it used to be and his skin much darker. But his shoulders were still broad and legs lean. What changed the most was his expression. It was dangerous. Sullen. Of a man that had known pain, though he would admit it to no one.

I was escorted beneath a large atrium, past endless portraits and embroidered settees. A clear *clack clack* echoed out as my new silver tipped cane struck the floor.

Entering the dining room was entering a world of crimson silk damask. Massive paintings of dead kings and queens stared at me as I walked down the length of the table. The chatter of the guests died into silence. I only heard their necks cracking as they craned in unnatural positions just to catch a glimpse of me as I passed.

A chair was pulled out and I was glad to take my seat, relieving the pain already pounding in my ankle. Unfortunately, that seat was beside Octavia.

The king stood at the end of the table, and a rustle of shifting fabric and scooting chairs followed. I cursed having already to rise.

"Tonight, we are joined by Mr. Ross Daltry. A soldier of His Majesty's army. He has taken a pledge and given his word to both God and his king to solve the mystery that baffles our court. We toast him and wish him well on his quest," the king said, lifting a glass of champagne.

Applause rippled through the crowded table. I took a small bow and sat back down. I did not need their false praise or worthless wishes.

Doors flung open as a rush of servants wearing wigs that resembled cement carried in large silver platters. They were placed on the table and the lids removed revealing culinary creations of simmering quails, towers of eggs, and mouthwatering soups. Conversation exploded along with clinking glasses and violins.

A gloved servant sat a small tray before me and removed the lid revealing frog legs soaked in cream. Madeira wine filled my glass. Only then I felt the greatness of my hunger.

I tore the flesh from the delicate bones with ease and

called for more wine. I grabbed an egg for good measure, though it was not nearly as exciting as the caramelized quail I sunk my teeth into.

Octavia only picked at her quail. She expertly sliced through the flesh, the few bites she took no bigger than a pea. She barely sipped her wine. The other nobles were similar, allowing the food prepared for them to sit and congeal as they spoke of hunting and silk ribbons.

A giggle broke through my revulsion. Looking through the forest of silver candlesticks Aurelia and a dandy passed amused glances at me. Whispers of my name carried through the chorus of clanging dishes and cutting knives. Several fine ladies wearing large feathers in their hair pointed in my direction. I knew they were discussing bets if I would survive. The lives of the common were always viewed as sport.

My cravat grew hot and sweat collected at my temples. The vest constricted, and I could barely move in the tight jacket. I took another large swig of wine, savoring the calm heat running through me.

"How long were you in service to the army?" Octavia asked, her voice shocking me back.

I didn't wish to answer. All they were after was for something more to mock. I speared a thick slice of roast beef and laid it on my plate, making sure my eyes never left the prongs.

"Father told us you fought at the Battle of Dunlap," she said again, trying to bully me into conversation. Nobles always believed they deserved what they wanted.

I couldn't hold my tongue any longer.

"In court it may be common to gossip about this and that, but in my world, one is trained to be silent, Your Highness," I stated coolly.

A pause followed.

"I meant no ill will," she said.

I answered by slicing through the tender flesh, but my

fork fell from my grip and clanged against the silver plate. She held my wrist firm and definite. Fire burned up my arm, and heat stirred in my breeches. She was either determined, or insufferable.

My gaze shot to hers. Pleading riddle her blue eyes and something else I didn't recognize, but wished to alleviate. What was wrong with me?

"Father is a man of exaggeration," she whispered. She gripped me tighter. Her pulse pounded through her palm. "I assure you we are innocent of the crimes we have been accused."

My skin blazed as she kept her hold. I saw through her, though my body betrayed me. She was using her charms against me. I knew the sort of woman she was. A flicker of the eyes, a pout of the lips, and I would be putty in her hands.

I ripped my wrist from her claws almost knocking over my glass of Madeira. Her heat still lingered on my skin.

"Your shoes speak otherwise, Your Highness," I hissed.

Her expression darkened.

"You think us criminals when the true crime is the bloodshed Father spills vanquishing this mad desire," she said, indignant. "We are obedient daughters and must honor his wishes though it displeases us."

She sipped at her wine.

"Why do you not tell him how your shoes become destroyed if this upsets you so?" I asked.

"Father will not accept reason. He will not accept that you will find there is no mystery. There is no secret. Just as Prince Jonathan discovered before he met the blade," she said, a sob threatening at the back of her throat. "Do you not fear death to take this mad adventure?"

I smirked.

"Death is only something to fear if you have something to lose," I replied.

"This is a matter of bravery, then," she said. "A fool's belief."

"Bravery is for children," I shot back. "I speak of philosophy."

Disappointment pulled down on her pink lips.

"Philosophy will not save you from the guillotine. You should never have come. There is a madness about the king and madness and philosophy never mix. I suggest you leave while you still can. I will calm the king's anger and you can avoid what will be a certain death."

She was a grand little vixen.

"Is that what you told the others?" I spat.

"Others?" she asked. Her brows furrowed and she bit her cheek.

"Your father said there were other challengers that simply went missing," I snapped. Her cheeks reddened and her breasts rose and fell quickly as if nervous. "I suppose you helped them escape. In the army, that would have been treason and you would have been hung from the next tree."

It was only then I realized how close I had moved towards her. Her breath was hot against my skin and she smelled of rose water and fine powder. Her eyes narrowed and she pressed her lips together as she turned away.

I quickly sat back against my chair, wishing my pounding heart would slow.

KING RUPERT RETIRED to his chambers with a giggling woman whose rouge matched the damask chairs. It was made clear I was to stay with the princesses and their fops. Cards and brandy were suggested in the salon.

Three of the princesses sat on blue satin settees embroidering handkerchiefs. One played a Mozart sonata at the piano forte. Another drew with charcoal beside the marble fireplace. Several others leaned against the yellow silk walls engrossed in conversations with men whose high collars almost engulfed their chins. The rest played cards and passed entire fortunes back and forth across the green felted table. Octavia was among them.

I refused to join in these games, even though their protestations grew quite passionate. I remained standing in a far corner, passing the time reading the titles of books that had never been opened in a good century.

"Your new knight is not as fun as the other princes," a man complain over the sound of stacking chips. "Won't even fancy a game of whist! I can't imagine being so dull as to pass up a game of whist."

I pulled a volume of Voltaire from the shelf trying to ignore him and thumbed through the stiff pages.

"Let him be, William," Henrietta's sharp voice replied. "Not everyone enjoys entertainment. Mr. Daltry is much too clever for us. That is why he prefers brooding."

My skin bristled with their giggles as they reshuffled their deck of cards.

"Perhaps if he had spent more time playing cards, he wouldn't need that cane," another man said.

A playful slap echoed out followed by more laughter. I tried to focus on the words of the book, but I already read the same sentence over five times. Or perhaps it was seven.

"Still, you have to admire the freedom he must have," Sophia added. "He doesn't have to bother with stuffy events or treaties. You remember my cousin, the Duchess of Fenway? Such a pretty thing. What straight teeth! All wasted. She was sent to some ungodly little kingdom in the far northern isles, and wed to a man three times her age and four times her size!"

"Speak for yourself!" Matilda said. "I'd take such a marriage if it meant never having to wear corsets again."

They complained about their bejeweled lifestyle, yet I doubted they would complain of whale bone when their toes snapped from frostbite or bellies rumbled with hunger. I chuckled to myself imagining her scrubbing her own chamber pot. If she wanted a new life I would be happy to oblige her once I was king.

"Daltry!"

The lovely thought vanished and I snapped my book shut. I turned around facing William, a man who looked as bright as a pig and roughly the same size. His pink suit pulled awkwardly at his elbows and knees, and three gold buttons threatened to pop off his vest.

"What is it?" I asked through gritted teeth.

"The man has no manners!" the other exclaimed. He resembled the scarecrows that stood stiff and frozen in corn fields, his nose hooked and eyes small and vacant of thought. "That is the Duke of Brambly, Sir. And I am the Duke of Kilton. If you are to address us, you will do so only with 'Your Grace'."

I hadn't wished to kill a man so intensely in years, but I hardly thought the king would appreciate me filleting one of his nobles when my own position was still precarious. No, I had better wait until after my position was secure. Then, I could come up with more satisfying tortures.

"Excuse me, what is it, *Your Grace?*" I growled, imagining his toes roasting over hot coals.

"It seems to me if you are to stay among these delightful ladies, we should know a little more about you," the scarecrow said. "Charlotte tells me you were a soldier? Sounds fascinating."

He crossed his knee, his green pinstripe suit lengthening his thin body further.

"The king is satisfied with my history," I said.

His eyes narrowed and his slender lips curled into a devilish smile.

"I do not doubt it, but, indulge us," he said. The ridiculousness of his entire person vanished, replaced by cold menace.

I could sense the ears of the others burning. Their conversations grew quiet, even the light notes of the keyboard had silenced. Damn if I would allow a man whose cravat of bows was thicker than his own neck intimidate me.

"You answered your own question," I hissed. "I was a soldier, and now I am not. What riveting gossip."

William leaned forward, his pink collar scraping his fat cheeks.

"So much information, Mr. Daltry, and yet so little," he said. His gaze crackled with malice.

"A man of mystery!" the scarecrow added.

My grip tightened on my cane. I wouldn't be able to contain my anger much longer.

"Let Mr. Daltry be," Octavia commanded.

"My dear, this man is to share your chambers," William protested. "Surely, you can't be so blasé about this? The others have all been princes for God's sake. This man has eaten in trenches with rats."

I saw only red, and my heart pounded for revenge. My lip curled as I walked right before him, his fat thighs rolling off either side of his chair. I was going to make this pig squeal.

Towering above him I lifted my cane and pressed the end into the base of his fat throat. He grabbed hold of the stick and tried to shove it away, but I only pushed harder until he gasped for breath.

"Sir, I assure you the rats were better company than you," I said. A sickly tinge of purple started to infect his face and I couldn't stop a thrill rushing through me.

"How dare you!" the scarecrow exclaimed, standing to his feet. He tried to grab my arm, but I easily threw him back.

"What are you going to do?" I asked with a chuckle.

William tried to shove my cane away, but I lunged it even deeper until his pink tongue rolled out of his mouth.

"I could have you thrown in prison for this," the scarecrow said, his voice cutting through my rush.

I removed my cane, and William rubbed his throat while coughing like an old hag. He was right and anger boiled within me. Even as the king's champion I would always be a plebeian. A mortal among false gods.

The scarecrow laughed and sat back in his chair. He swirled his brandy and took a sip as if it had all been a capital joke.

"The king seems to be losing his touch," he said to the princesses. "That man is a wild dog."

"Hush now," Henrietta scolded.

He would not be contained.

"Couldn't even find a proper soldier," he continued. "Look at that limp. Pathetic."

My teeth ground together.

"Insufferable!" William rasped. "I would never lower myself to be injured in battle."

"You'd never be allowed in battle," the scarecrow mocked. He dared me now to fight again. They both did.

"Still, I would have the brains enough to get out of the way," William said. "Damn inconvenient to waste a surgeon's time due to your lack of dexterity."

"Enough!"

The room went silent.

Octavia stood. Her eyes were wild and her skin flushed red. She resembled a feral animal. My heart tumbled, but out of fear of her, or *for* her, I didn't know. Didn't want to know.

The two dimwits' mouths opened wide and blubbed like

dying fish on a dock.

"Gentlemen," she said, her voice cold. "Mr. Daltry is a retired soldier of the crown. He is to be shown only our gratitude for having fought for the kingdom. He is a man of bravery. You do I and my sisters a disservice speaking of him in such a cruel manner, especially in our presence."

My lips nearly went slack myself.

The eleven other sisters rose from their places and stepped by her side, standing as a force no one dared cross.

"Come now, Octavia," the scarecrow stuttered. "Mr. Daltry knows it was all in jest."

Her eyes narrowed.

"All in jest?" She asked, her voice lowering. Growling. "Perhaps the lands and titles you have been granted were all in jest. Mr. Daltry is the king's chosen champion and currently his heir. Your future king. I suggest if you enjoy your current luxuries you apologize. Now."

Their lips quivered, and they dug their fingers between their necks and cravats.

"It...appears we have spoken out of turn," William croaked to me.

"Quite right," the scarecrow said. "Please accept our... heartfelt...apologies."

I grunted, not knowing what else to do. I was unaccustomed to those of high birth coming to my aide, and now I had twelve princesses who demanded I be treated with respect.

I needed to leave. Before I left through the double doors, I dared a short glance at Octavia. She smiled sweetly, and I had the odd sensation as if everything would be all right. Guilt washed the warm feeling away, reminding me of how rude I had been myself towards her earlier.

Clearing my throat from the tightness that gripped it, I escaped into the dimly lit halls.

CHAPTER 4

I held tightly onto my satchel and waited. I tapped my fingers against the arm of my chair as my eyes stayed locked on the gilded clock ticking beside me. The clock struck ten. Then, an hour after ten. My fingers drummed harder. The sooner I could get this business over with, the sooner I could claim the fate awaiting me.

The hinges of a door creaked open, and a servant motioned me to follow him. Thank God. He led me back through the three hallways, beneath the atrium that was taller than a church, up those damned stairs that caused my ankle to grind and throb.

"This is where you will stay, Sir," the servant said as we entered a lavish side chamber. An embroidered chair sat pushed hard against a wall of sprawling golden motifs. "You will be able to see everything from here should anything go amiss."

I saw quickly what he meant. The chair faced a room of heavy wardrobes, twelve four-poster beds, and twelve women readying for the night. The only privacy the princesses received were several screens they hid behind to change.

They tossed their silk gowns over the sides and flung their shoes creating tumbling piles. Octavia sat at her vanity without reserve combing her blonde hair in counted strokes.

Heat flushed down my chest as I couldn't help but imagine running my fingers through her soft curls. I bit the inside of my lip willing the image to vanish. This was highly irregular witnessing such an intimate scene, but I had little recourse. The servant pointed at the chair and only left after I took my post as knight and guardian.

My ankle split into a spasm, and a grunt escaped my lips from deep within my stomach. I bent down and clutched my leg, pressing my thumb into the coiling muscle. I tried to stretch it out, but it refused to bend. I was an invalid and for a full minute I believed myself insane for ever believing I was capable of becoming a king.

Remain brave, strong, and true, and all will unravel as it should...

A shadow fell over me. I looked up seeing Octavia holding a blanket, her face twisted with concern.

"What can I do?" she asked. "Doctor Closett is quite exceptional. He could offer you relief."

She knelt down by my feet and tried to help me stretch out the cramp.

"That won't be necessary," I said, moving my ankle just out of her reach. A sting from such a sudden movement forced me to wince. Annoyance darkened her features and she shook her head.

"But you're in pain, and that is unacceptable to me," she said.

"I am used to it," I replied. I tried to force my lips into a reassuring smile, but she wasn't believing my lie.

"The palace can get chilly at night," she said, standing. "If you refuse the good sense of a doctor's help, you can at least take this for warmth."

Before I could protest she flapped the soft blanket open

and let it drape over my lap. My heart twisted in confusion. Loretta, my once betrothed, had left me to fend for myself when I had returned crippled from battle. Seeing I was of no use she made damn well sure she returned the favor, crushing my heart in the process. Now, a princess worried herself making sure I had every comfort I required.

Guilt sickened me again.

"Thank you," I said, the words grating in my throat.

"It's nothing, really," she said, smoothing out the wrinkles.

"Not for the blanket," I said. "For...earlier. In the salon."

Her blue eyes snapped up to meet my own and she rubbed her hand on top of mine. I gulped as her heat rippled through my body. I didn't try to remove my hand from her touch this time. I wanted it to remain connected to her forever, though I didn't know why.

"I abhor rudeness," she said. "William and Felix had no right to speak to you in such an odious manner. You think us all enemies, but some of us do have hearts that beat for those other than ourselves. We cannot help we were born into a life of plenty, no more than those born to a life of ash and smoke."

Her words stung. I wanted to hate her, but I was finding it increasingly more difficult.

She removed her hand just as Matilda approached. She held a silver tray with a pitcher and a goblet. If you had told me Matilda had been chiseled from fine marble I would have believed you. Each cheekbone was hard and perfectly rounded, while her lips remained perpetually content.

Matilda placed the tray down on a table beside me and poured me a goblet of wine. An aroma of plum and cedar caused my mouth to water. The pounding tendons in my ankle also desired the warm relief it promised.

Octavia's shoulders tightened as she watched the goblet pass from her sister's hand to mine. Matilda's gaze intensified.

"See, we do not all rejoice in the trials of others," Matilda said, cocking her head to the side. Her rigid skin cracked as her lips twisted.

"Let's leave him alone," Octavia said, her voice chilled. Worry seemed to float behind her eyes, but she quickly hid it away as she pulled on her sister's arm. "Goodnight, Mr. Daltry."

With a deep curtsy they both left and returned to their rooms, where the other ten princesses were already in their beds. Octavia and Matilda extinguished the remaining candles and wedged themselves beneath thick duvets.

My only source of light was a single candlestick beside me. The wine was black in the shadows, but that didn't put me off in the slightest. I lifted the goblet to my mouth. It was cold as it touched my lips.

"Ow!" I breathed quietly.

A sting flashed over my upper leg. Digging into my pockets my fingertips hit something sharp. Angular. Pulling it out a metal crucifix dangled from its chain.

It had seen me through much, and while I was not one for religion or superstition, I never could bring myself to throw it out. I dove it into my coat pocket instead, but as I did, some of the wine slipped over the rim and spilled onto my shirt.

"Dammit," I whispered.

Retrieving my handkerchief I tried to soak up the spill. The wine shimmered in the candlelight, and as I pulled the cloth through the crimson liquid the aroma changed. The fragrance of currant and earth deepened into something caustic. Bitter.

Familiar.

My heart quickened as I lifted the goblet to my nose and smelled deeply. I was back in the battlefield. Shapes twisted and curved. A doctor told me I would feel better after I drank from his cup.

Laudanum.

The other princes hadn't failed from being weak, they had failed from being drugged.

I turned to the small flame and blew it out, shrouding myself in darkness. Trying not to make a sound, I groped beneath the table until my fingertips touched something hard and cold. I pulled out the chamber pot and peeled back the linen cloth. I poured the wine inside and re-covered the rim, placing it back beneath the table and returning the empty goblet to the silver tray.

The rustling of sheets crinkled in my ears. My heart pounded. Light flickered in the princesses' room.

I closed my eyes and leaned back in my chair, taking in heavy breaths that bordered on snores. If they wanted me asleep, then that is what I had to be.

They approached me, their feet pattering almost silently along the inlaid wooden floor. A yellow flame neared my face. It's heat kissed my skin and glowed through my closed eyelids.

"Is he asleep?" Camilla asked just above a whisper.

"Looks that way," Aurelia replied.

One tapped my boot. Another poked my shoulder. Still I kept my breaths deep and even.

"Men are so gullible," Matilda laughed. "Willing to risk their lives for a bit of drink or skirt. Idiotic creatures."

"Still, there is something different about this one. He isn't like the others," Aloysia added. I felt her fingers comb through my hair. "He's so...old."

"Pish-posh," Octavia said. "Age only serves to make a man more interesting. It is a true shame he should end up like the rest. I had hoped...He should never have taken father's challenge."

Her words were uncommonly bitter. I cracked my eyes

ever so slightly and saw her pick up the empty goblet and examine the inside.

"All men are the same" Charlotte replied, taking it from her grasp and setting it back on the tray. "Well, except for a select few."

They giggled as if it were some inside joke they shared. The light floated away as their voices grew faint and I dared open my eyes.

Their braids unraveled and a thousand pins latched their curls firmly in place. Corsets were retied and vibrant gowns cascaded down their chemises. Rouge and powder rolled in clouds off their white skin.

Sophia turned the little golden key of the largest wardrobe and flung the doors open. Inside was nothing but shoes. Blue. Pink. Purple. Satin. Silk. Lace. Heeled. Flat. Each sister stood before the shelves of cascading ribbons and shimmering jewels and chose which they liked best. Sliding their feet into the luxurious fabrics they clicked along the wooden floor.

Caroline smoothed the wrinkles of her dress, while Amelia twirled and Sophia gave a deep curtsy as if practicing for a ball. Octavia swayed between them, her silk gown of deep blue sweeping the floor. She stood tall before the largest four-poster bed. The others gathered behind her, forming a tidy single file line.

Closing her eyes, she hovered her hands out on either side of her for a second or two and then brought them together in a loud clap.

Gears ground together and metal scraped metal. The bed rustled and shook, then sunk an inch at a time below the floor. All that remained was a large, hollow space. I wanted to move to see better, but I dared not.

Octavia descended first, followed by Matilda, then Amelia and Sophia, the line trailing from oldest to youngest.

Caroline drifted down as if it were a promenade. Aloysia took three steps then stopped.

Her shoulders stiffened. My breath refused to come.

She craned her neck slowly towards me until her eyes locked on mine. Or at least, I thought they did. I forced my body to remain frozen as her lids fluttered trying to see me through the dark. My heart pounded until it burned within my chest.

Her arms relaxed. She turned away, her slender form disappearing beneath the floor.

I sighed in relief, though my relief didn't last long. Gears quaked. The floor vibrated. Even the pitcher threatened to topple from the table as the entrance started to seal.

I had seconds.

Grabbing my cane and my satchel I quickly hobbled towards the closing door. The metal scraped in my ears. Chains rattled and screeched. I hastened my pace. My ankle strained in agony. The muscle was tearing. It didn't matter. I gritted my teeth and kept forward. The door fell several more inches. My leg wanted to give way. My ankle throbbed as if ready to snap. I leaned into my cane refusing it the pleasure.

I couldn't let it. Wouldn't.

Just as the door was an inch from closing I shoved my cane between the thin gap. The gears stopped. The chains fell silent.

Bending down I grabbed hold of the heavy door and pried it up, just enough so I could slip inside. A seemingly endless spiral staircase awaited me, the vibrant colors of silk swirling down past black rock. I started to retrieve my cane, but as I inspected the mechanisms my stomach pitted. I would have no way to open it again. My cane would have to be abandoned.

A rush of cool air rustled through my hair as I looked

down again. The last glimmer of Aloysia's purple gown disappeared from view.

I had no choice.

Opening my satchel I pulled out the delicate cloak and threw it over my shoulders. It slipped against my skin as I covered my head. Looking down I chilled at nothing but the gray stone steps. I was utterly invisible. The Oracle had gifted me a miracle.

Biting my lip I took that first, excruciating step down. A piercing crick flashed through every bone and tendon. My breath stuck in my throat and I was glad for it as it drowned out a grunt. I ground my fingers into the mortar of the stone for support as I kept down. My limbs shook and my stomach wanted to retch as the pain tore through me. I kept on.

A glint of purple caught my eye and I focused my every strength on the shade.

Down I continued until I believed I was entering the belly of hell. The color grew larger. Closer. Until I could smell the scent of lavender and musk rising from Aloysia's skin. I followed ten paces behind, thankful the chorus of their heeled shoes striking the steps drowned out the faltering of my own.

The torment enveloped my entire leg now. I was rigid, but I kept my eyes firmly on the purple fabric flicking up off the ground with every step Aloysia took.

However, the farther we descended, the less sharp the pain became. I found I didn't need to grip the stones so tightly. In fact, I didn't have to grip them at all. I was standing taller, straighter. A rush of energy flowed through my every muscle. I felt twenty years younger.

There was no pain at all. My right ankle was just as sound as the left. Where were we? I didn't question the reason. There was little time for that. I scurried down the remaining steps jumping over the last two for good measure. When I looked out, I almost shielded my eyes.

White. Bright and burning.

A grove of silver trees split up through silver earth. I stopped and stared in wonder at the hardened leaves. They shimmered prettily beneath a silver sun, and I hardly noticed myself reaching for the metallic branches.

"Keep up, ladies. We can't keep them waiting," Aurelia's voice cut through the spell.

I retracted my arm and shook my head. The marvels didn't end there. The trees of silver led into a woodland of gold and the woodland of gold bled into a forest of diamonds. The leaves glistened as stars, every vein and ripple encrusted with the glittering jewels.

I forced each foot before the other to keep pace with the princesses as they wove between the lavish trees. I couldn't peel my eyes away from the stunning wealth surrounding me. Anger quickly boiled in my veins. I knew how they paid for their shoes. In this secret land there were riches enough to feed an entire world, yet they kept it for themselves to buy a bit of ribbon and silk.

They stopped.

A black lake spread out before us, a castle glowing white rising behind it. The light from the windows shimmered across the water. Octavia approached the lake's edge as if it were the most common thing to do. Hiking up her skirts she bent down, placing her pink palm flat atop the water's surface.

Golden orbs neared the shore like beacons on a black sea. I squinted through the gloom. Gray silhouettes of men in rowboats immerged, their oars slicing through the glistening water in fast strokes. Twelve in all. The sand crumbled as the edge of their boats cut into the shore.

They hopped out, their heeled shoes sinking into the

mud. They gave a low bow, crowns of gold glimmering within their hair. They were young and strapping, dressed in fine suits with collars tight and high. One particularity they all shared was how they gazed at the princesses as if goddesses of Mount Olympus.

Octavia took the extended hand of a blonde prince. His angular jaw was fierce, and his eyes made you believe he feared nothing. He easily lifted her into the boat and jumped back in himself. He shoved off from the shore, his oars effortlessly cutting into the black.

I watched the same pattern occur down the line. Matilda chose a broad shouldered fellow, while Sophia one thin and angular. Dorothea preferred a man with a fine scar trailing from right eyebrow to left cheek.

As always, Aloysia was last. I had but seconds to make my move.

"My princess," the young man said, his manicured hand waiting for hers. His red hair was neatly tied with a black ribbon. The strength of his jaw and cheekbones showed him a man, but his green eyes continued to shine with youthful naïvety.

He gripped around her trim waist and lifted her into the boat. I followed, but cursed inwardly as my feet made a distinct thud against the wooden boards. The boat rocked, sending ripples across the water.

"Theodore, do be careful," she said. "I cannot afford to have my gown wet."

She examined her skirts making sure a rogue drop hadn't already laid waste to the fabric.

"A thousand apologies, my princess," he replied. "I shall be more careful. Your comfort is my only desire."

He sounded deranged, but you would have to be deranged to wear such a high collar as he.

She nodded her head and flipped open her fan. Knees

bent, he pushed the boat off the bank and jumped inside. I was wedged between them, trying to keep my breathing as shallow as possible.

Lanterns bobbed all around us and in the distance a majestic sight. A castle of glistening towers rose on the horizon, white turrets surging into the night sky. That alone should have been enough to shake my soul, but it was the music swelling the silence that gripped me.

Bows of violins glided across thin strings, while a harpsichord plucked a dark melody. My heart wanted to leap along with the spiraling notes. The music wanted to consume me. I wanted it to consume me.

My right hand was tapping my lap with the beat. I clapped the other on top of it to stop. Still, my fingertips tingled. Even my toes. A rush of energy washed over me, as if time stopped and youth was eternal. All I had to do was dance.

I pushed the overwhelming desire away, the sensation splintering into oblivion. I was here on business and could not risk distraction.

I nearly fell face first into the prince's lap as the boat came to a sudden halt. He Leapt out of the boat and tied a rope around a post of the dock. Eleven identical boats floated empty beside us.

"My lady, the dance awaits," he said. He extended his hand to Aloysia. She snapped her fan shut and took his hand with glee, leaving me a stranger in a kingdom underground.

ONCE I WAS certain they would not hear me, I disembarked and flew down the dock. My feet pounded the wooden boards without pain. I was running. Free. Air slunk across my skin and filled my lungs and I never wanted the exhilaration to cease. Spiraling hedges flicked by and lanterns burned high overhead.

Only when I reached a set of large doors did I stop. Catching my breath, I grabbed the handles and threw them open. The sight inside I believed only existed between the pages of fairy tales.

Music shimmered as brightly as the revelers' clothing. Couples danced a waltz, the rhythm infecting your bones. It sizzled my toes and I caught myself starting to sway. Shoes slid along an immense polished floor beneath a painted ceiling. The princesses twirled as their princes' hands glided across their silk bodices.

I snuck through the ballroom, fighting the urge to dance that kept thrashing in my veins. Careful to avoid flying elbows, I wove between Aurelia and Henrietta. A gentleman's foot came perilously close to my own. I jumped to the left, nearly crashing into a youth carrying a platter of macarons and tarts.

I crept beside an ancient grandfather clock, thankful for the dull ticking that broke the enchantment of the melody.

Applause erupted at the end of each dance, and I noted there were more than twelve princes. At least sixty gentlemen waited along the edges of the ballroom. All wore the same golden crowns and dressed in the same tight fitting suits. All kept their gazes firmly on the princesses as if a lover.

I stepped away quickly as Caroline released her prince to the fold and curtsied before another man with thick black hair. He smiled as if seeing a sunrise for the first time and kissed her hand. This seemed to please her and she pulled him away where they joined the other spinning couples.

Curiosity getting the better of me I kept along the fringe. I wanted to see more of this odd place. I thought my heart stopped when I caught sight of Octavia.

She commanded them all. Power and grace exuded from

her every step and twirl. A broad shouldered man bowed and slid his hand behind her slim waist. Her lips parted into a smile. Her cheeks flushed a deeper shade.

I continued along the edge, careful as I maneuvered between the collection of men that stood like trees. I couldn't help my eyes falling to Octavia. She fell into the arms of an eager partner, only to spin away into the embrace of another.

A pearl fell from her shoe.

It rolled across the floor, passed the men's pointed leather boots and beside the princesses' pointed silk heels. It came to a rest right before me. Kneeling, I picked up the smooth orb and placed it deep within my pockets.

A pink ribbon twirled by followed by a split heel.

The dance continued.

The clock chimed one. The clock chimed two.

Shreds of silk trailed behind the princesses' spinning feet. Lace was torn and toes peeked through growing holes. Still they danced. The music grew feverish. It infected my bones and my entire body vibrated with the dark melody. It wanted me to join.

It needed me...

I shook it away, focusing on the glittering hail falling from their shoes. Diamonds, gold, and emeralds bounced off the marble floor and rolled beneath cracking soles. Buckles snapped. Seams popped. Strips of fabric disintegrated before my eyes.

Their cheeks were red and lips plump, almost as if they were drunk. They tugged the jackets of their princes, forcing them closer against their heaving bosoms. The men leaned their faces against their cheeks, their arms and hands skating down every arc and sinew. Some kissed passionately.

I couldn't stop a rush of jealousy as the man with the scar ran his fingers up Octavia's neck and into her hair. She laughed musically.

BONG! BONG! BONG!

I covered my ears. Every clock chimed three as if summoning the horsemen of the apocalypse.

The music ceased. The dance stopped. The princesses were escorted back towards the boats, leaving the remnants of their shoes behind.

My heart raced. I ran across the emptying ball room, careful not to trip on an errant ruby or broken buckle. My only hope to avoid discovery was to board the first boat with Octavia.

I squeezed beside the princes and princesses as they filed out of the doors, but in my haste I came too close to Henrietta's skirts. My shoe tugged on the silk and a distinct rip tore over their chatter.

"Look what you did, Bertram!" Henrietta scolded her prince.

"A thousand apologies, Your Grace," he said. "But my foot was nowhere near your gown."

"It didn't tear by itself," she snapped.

She pointed at the frayed fabric. He just bowed his head in surrender like a dog to its master.

"I told you, there is something odd about this place tonight," Aloysia piped. "I've felt watched all evening."

I froze.

"You've been reading far too many novels," Octavia said. "We can't waste time worrying about phantoms."

As they stood in debate, I took the opportunity to slide past them. Their feet thundered behind me as we traveled back through the twisting bushes and to the dock. Octavia stepped in the first boat, and I slunk in quickly after.

I dared not breath the whole time, and my mind kept swirling with splitting shoes and dark melodies.

Once we hit shore, I jumped out at the first available moment and ran. I sprinted back up the bank and through the diamond forest. Their voices were never far behind, causing me to quicken my pace even more.

I ducked beneath a low hanging golden branch. Swiped past the silver leaves, the faintest rustle echoing out in my wake.

Laughter bubbled behind me. I forced myself to move even faster.

I raced up the stairs, skipping two at a time. My lungs started to burn and my heart pounded into my throat. The breath of youth I experienced withered away. The pain returned. My ankle ground into the surrounding tendons. Bones cracked and muscle coiled.

Sweat ran down my temples. My ankle could no longer support my weight. I gripped the stone walls, plunging into the cracks and crevices to help pull myself along. Ten steps I counted, each agony. My nails split as I dug them deeper into the mortar.

Throbbing and pounding, my ankle snapped beneath my weight. I collapsed onto the stairs.

Voices. Laughter. They were right up behind me now.

Before me the faintest light escaped from the crack where my cane still remained lodged between the floor and the door. I sucked in a deep breath and stifled a cry of pain. My hands scratched across the stone steps as I pulled myself up the stairs. I dug my knees into the rock and pushed with my left foot. Gravel stuck to the hot liquid covering my palms.

The light grew stronger. I pushed harder. My ankle throbbed, but I couldn't let it be my ruin.

I grabbed for my cane, my fingers barely scraping the smooth surface. Their footsteps echoed up the spiral staircase. Seconds were all I had. I made one last effort. My fingers curled around the cane, and in one swift movement I placed it under my arm and pushed the door open with my shoulders.

I rolled over across the floor, letting the door close shut behind me.

Hobbling and trembling, I limped across the marble floor. Removing the cloak, I stuffed it in my bag and threw it beneath the table. Just as I fell into my empty seat the door creaked open and voices filled the silence.

My breaths could not be caught. I hungered for air, but I couldn't gasp as I wished. My shirt was cold with sweat.

I almost lost my composure when a warm hand touched my forehead.

"Is he ill?" Amelia asked.

"He doesn't have a fever," Camilla replied, removing her touch.

"He looks like death," Caroline added. "Look how heavy he is breathing."

"Let him be," Octavia said.

A soft cloth dabbed across my forehead. Rose water radiated from Octavia's heated skin.

"He is having a nightmare, that is all. Quite common for someone who has seen war," she added. "Poor man. I hate he should survive battle only to meet his fate at father's doing."

The sweet scent enraptured me. I wanted to inhale deeper, but the cloth was removed.

They trailed away, removing hair pins and gowns. Duvets were thrown back and silk slipped against linen as they slid between their sheets. Once I was sure they were asleep, I opened my eyes.

Tattered shoes were thrown outside their door in a pile.

The melody swirled in my mind like a ghost.

I dove into my pocket and gripped my crucifix. I pressed its sharp points into my fingers, needing it to ground me. To remind me where I was.

I was here. In King Rupert's castle, not below ground in a kingdom of midnight dances.

CHAPTER 5

"Lies!" the king spat. His face contorted into disgust as he looked me in the eye.

"I never lie, Sire," I said. I lengthened my body and tightened my lips together so I wouldn't bare my teeth.

"You expect me to believe your twisted tales? An underground kingdom? An army of princes? Drugging the wine? The whole thing is ridiculous," he snarled.

His breath smelled of brandy and every line on his face aged him by twenty years. The redness infecting his cheeks flushed down his neck. Even his hands that were curled tight were pink with rage. I wouldn't back down from such intimidation. Not when my word was being questioned.

He turned away and walked to the window and stared out, drumming his fingers on the ledge of gold.

"I understand your misgivings, but that is what I saw," I said.

His fingers stilled.

"Is it?" he mocked. "Are you sure it isn't just the creations of a coward afraid of the scaffold?"

He faced me once more, sneering. My grip tightened on

42

my cane hating how his accusations cut deeper than I imagined.

"I am no coward," I hissed.

He looked back out his window and waved me away as if bored. I refused to leave so easily. This man had me take a pledge, one I upheld, and now he was trying to steal my chance away. Damn him and his whole lot thinking they could always steal their promised rewards if the answer displeased them.

I lurched towards him, rage hot in my veins.

"I have proof," I snapped.

I dug into my pocket and retrieved the pearl that snapped off Octavia's shoe. He snatched it out of my fingers, inspected it for two seconds then threw it across the room. It clucked off the wall.

"That proves nothing," he hissed. Everything about him trembled.

He was maddening. Mad. Perhaps he *was* mad.

"I've done everything you've asked," I said, my words squeezed between gritting teeth. "I watched the princesses and followed them. I saw their shoes rip to pieces. The pearl I just now presented you was cast from one of them. I have fulfilled my word."

He glared at me and I saw murder burning behind his pupils.

"You've bitten off more than you can chew. You're just trying to get out of your oath. Fool the old man. Give him a worthless bauble and a fantastic tale. That should quell his curiosity," he shouted. "I won't be fooled so easily."

Anger ripped through me he should be so untrusting. I did what he asked, but as usual, it was never enough. When it came time to pay, there were always loopholes or addendums. I was but a king's toy and right now he was becoming bored.

"I swear on my honor as a soldier, what I say is true. I

gave you my oath. I have never broken my word and I don't intend to now," I said. "I would sooner die."

His right eye twitched.

"If you expect me to believe what you say, I need something a bit more convincing than a pearl. You claim this world is so fantastical, and then bring me something fantastic. Something I could never find in this kingdom," he said.

I bowed in acquiescence, my body fighting against such an act. He waved me away and I was all but happy to comply.

"Always thinking they are the maker of men's destinies," I grumbled as the doors shut behind me.

I wove back through the labyrinthine halls and rooms. Nobles sauntered lazily. Their soft voices grew louder as I passed. Ladies ducked behind their fans, though I could feel their prying eyes follow me.

"He will lose his head just as the others," one whispered.

The walls became narrow. The air thickened and grew hot. Sweat collected on my back. The rooms and halls had shrunk to half its size.

"The king is mad," another murmured. "That is certain."

"Are you sure? I thought the daughters wicked," another added, the mumbles gaining in numbers.

"The king has spilt so much blood," they all echoed.

I ran hot fingers through my hair. My pace quickened, though not as fast as I would have wished. Not as swift as I could move in the kingdom below with my crippled ankle. A bow fell down over thin strings. The music returned in my mind and it told me I would be far better below.

I had to get out.

I flung open a set of French doors and escaped into the outdoors. The music ceased. The fresh air was cool against my heated skin. I walked across the golden gravel path and into the green fields just to the right. There was a small grove of trees hidden away. I leaned my back against the rough bark and tried to breathe calming breaths.

I wiped the sweat from my forehead and looked out across the wild lawn. Matilda and Sophia walked arm in arm, hats with ostrich feathers bending in the wind. Aurelia played shuttlecocks with that bastard Felix. I turned wanting to avoid them, but was stopped by a sight I did not expect.

Octavia sat on a lone bench of stone beside a tall hedge. She was so far removed from the others. Her white muslin gown clung to her legs allowing one to see every dip and arc. I couldn't help that irritating flash of heat coil in my breeches.

She tore off jagged bits of a maple leaf and watched as the green fell on her lap. The vivaciousness she wore only yesterday was replaced by a somber look I had seen too many times. Often in my own reflection.

It was of lost hope.

Before I realized what I was doing, I approached her. My mouth was opening and soft words fell out of my mouth unhindered.

"Try not to dwell on it, or else it becomes all you think of," I said.

She turned to me, wiping a stray tear from her cheek.

"I'm afraid there is little else I can think of," she replied.

She brushed off the remnants of leaf that collected between her legs.

"What ails you?" I asked, incapable of stopping myself.

I was a right idiot. I should despise her, and yet, I wanted to comfort her. Help her. I ended up only despising myself.

"I dare say my troubles will only cause you laughter," she said, giving a tearful chuckle. "A man who has seen and faced death such as you will have no mercy for me."

Yesterday she would have been right. But today, at this moment, I was ashamed she thought me so cruel.

"Let me be the judge of that," I said.

She smiled, the red mist infecting her eyes slowly starting to disappear.

"Sit." She patted the empty spot and I sat beside her. Her gaze remained locked on her sisters frolicking in the distance. "I sometimes sit here and mourn the freedom we had as children. There was only the garden and the bedtime stories nurse read to us. Such lovely fairy tales..." she trailed off for a moment. "I am to be sent away. Married."

She said it so coldly as if they were the last words she would ever utter.

"I thought marriage was something to celebrate," I said, though I knew nothing of marriage.

She chuckled.

"Perhaps in your world, but in mine, marriages are contracts. Treaties. It is a union between countries, not of hearts."

My own heart grew heavy with pity for her.

"Who are you to marry?" My words were rougher than I expected.

"A king in Denmark who suffers from gout," she responded. "I will be wife number four. We are a bad match, but his kingdom can offer ours protection and a lifetime supply of herring."

Her pink, full lips quivered and the thought of some old fool kissing them became abhorrent to me.

I needed to leave. Everything I thought I knew spun. I made to get up, but her hand clapped over my wrist. Her heat smoldered my skin, and I was helpless to rip it away as I had before. I had no choice but to remain seated.

"How do you not dwell on your misfortunes?" she asked. "If I'm to take your advice, I'm afraid you must teach me."

Silence.

"I wander," I said. "As far as I can. If you never stay in one place, you can never think on your troubles."

She nodded as if she understood exactly what I meant.

"You find an escape," she echoed.

I had never thought about it in such a way, but she was right. My wandering and her midnight excursions were no different. Both were in desire to discover better worlds than the ones we currently resided.

"Yes," I said. "That is what led me here."

I tried to rise again, but a muscle coiled in my ankle. I fell back to the bench and grunted, gripping my cane until it passed.

"Are you sure you don't want me to fetch Dr. Closett?" she asked.

"No, they are nothing but professional quacks," I huffed. "I would have been better off dead then how they left me."

Her face twisted in curious confusion.

"What happened?" she asked.

I remained silent.

"I've shared my troubles with you, I think it only fair you return the favor," she said kindly. "As a future monarch and queen, I want to know the true cost of the wars we wage."

The chilled crust that contained me cracked at these words. She was the first to ever show any care. Most kings looked at their people as pawns on a chessboard. Black and white pieces that would fall, but never bleed. Here was a woman who truly wanted to understand the suffering they caused.

"It was twenty years ago," I started. "My regiment had been fighting at Dunlap for three weeks. The men who didn't starve to death succumbed to frostbite. The time came to attack, and we flew over the trenches. Through the frozen mud and dried blood. But it was too much...too...the enemy fired at us like a hell storm. One of my men fell to my right. A cannon ball exploded the earth before me. It took a man's head clean off his shoulders. Still we charged, stomachs empty, fingers so frozen we could barely pull the trigger to fire back."

She clapped her hand over her mouth. Tears rolled from her eyes again.

I continued.

"I lunged my bayonet. Musket balls spun past my ears. A blue uniformed soldier ran towards me, the whites of his eyes bright through the smoke and soot. I tried to bring my musket down on him, but…Pain. Pain enveloped my left side. My musket fell from my hand and sunk into the mud. Something was wet against my skin, hot and sticky. It ran down my stomach and drenched my skin. I continued towards the man, my hand firm against my side. I refused to die a coward.

"A pounding pressure tore through my ankle. I screamed out as I heard bone crack and shatter. My boot filled with blood. I fell to my knees and then to my hands. The snow was red. I collapsed. My world went black, but I could still hear. I could still hear as muskets fired and flesh burst. I could still hear the moans of dying men.

"I don't remember anything after that, except the doctor. His round spectacles sat on the tip of his thin nose. He told me he was saving my leg. That I was damn lucky to be alive. I would win a medal from the king for my bravery. That medal never paid for any food. Just a pretty trinket and a false sense of goodwill from the king. My bravery was forgotten as was I, as were we all."

I stopped, realizing I had never told a soul about that day. Octavia stared at me in horrified wonder.

"You asked me why I took the king's challenge," I continued. "That is why. Save the forgotten. Grant them a voice."

She squeezed my hand and I clapped mine over hers. I was grateful for her compassion in that moment.

"Mr. Daltry, I know you see us as two opposites. But we are similar in one way," she said.

I chuckled.

"How so?" I asked.

She looked back out at her sisters.

"We are both prisoners to the crown."

CHAPTER 6

We are both prisoners to the crown

I couldn't shake Octavia's words. Their chill.

That night as I waited for them to pretend to sleep, I gripped the crucifix in my hand. The sharp corners bit into my skin, and I enjoyed how each bite drove away the image of Octavia's sullen face. Drove away the music that lingered in my ears.

She acted like we were the same. That her plight was no different than mine.

Such a notion was ridiculous.

...Wasn't it?

Amelia's shadow fell over me. Her brown curls tumbled past angled shoulders, and her lean face was riddled with eagerness to please. She placed the same silver tray with the goblet and pitcher beside me.

She bent forward and poured wine into the goblet and held it out to me.

"Thank you." Inwardly I cursed her.

I placed the goblet back on the table. Her green eyes

flashed and her lips flattened. She lifted the goblet off the polished wood and handed it back to me.

"I wish you to taste it," she said. "It is different from last night and I would hate to leave you with a vintage that displeases you."

The aroma stung my nose and behind the fermented grapes the bitter scent of laudanum lingered. Stronger, this time.

"I am sure it will be satisfactory," I said, trying to sit it back on the tray.

She grabbed my wrist, hard, and lifted the goblet to my lips.

"I prefer you take a sip," she insisted.

Cold metal touched my lips as she tipped the cup forward. The wine splashed against my closed mouth, and it trickled down my chin. Fear burned my veins as her features barbed with cruel enjoyment.

She tilted the goblet higher and pressed it harder against my mouth forcing my lips to part. Warm wine flooded over my tongue and burned my throat.

Her slender form started to fade. I thought the chair moved beneath me. I drained all the wine.

She removed the goblet and blotted my lips with a soft, white handkerchief.

"That wasn't so hard, was it?" she asked.

I couldn't answer, only sway. She smiled and then kissed my forehead before leaving to join her sisters.

Haze already started to blur my vision. I couldn't succumb.

I tried to focus on anything that kept me grounded in the present. I counted the brush strokes they pulled through their hair. I pressed the crucifix deeper into my fingertips, though the sharp points were beginning to dull.

The candles extinguished. They slid between their silk

sheets and turned their backs to me. My veins were hot and pulsing. I fell to my knees against the wooden floor and grabbed the porcelain bedpan beneath the table. I retched into it, vacating my stomach entirely of the wretched wine.

My body weighed four hundred pounds as I wiped the vomit from my mouth and slunk back up to the chair. I leaned against the firm back, my head hitting the carved wood. My skin tingled, desiring sleep, and a fog still darkened my vision.

A candle light flickered in the gloom. I closed my eyes and my body sunk deeper into the chair. Sleep wanted to claim me. I wouldn't let it.

Footsteps neared me.

"I watched him drink it myself," Amelia said.

"Pity," Henrietta replied. "Octavia had so much hope for him."

Their voices swirled, but I held onto each note as if rocks on a sandy shore. Anything that kept me from falling away into the dregs of sleep.

"It is a shame it has to be this way," Amelia said.

They departed, their steps echoing loudly across the floorboards in my ears. I forced a heavy lid open. The candle-light was piercing and stung my pupils. I saw a storm of hair pins and cascading silks. Their voices chattered excitedly. Feet slid into shoes that sparkled and shined.

Clap! Clap! Clap!

It might have well been thunder.

Gears rumbled. Floorboards rattled. The princesses descended.

I had to follow.

I leaned heavily on my cane and stumbled towards the closing entry. The walls curved upwards, and the floor twisted to the right. I aimed for the staircase, fighting the fatigue causing my body to want to collapse.

Just as before I relinquished my cane to keep the door opened and covered myself in my cloak. If there was any benefit to the drug still pulsing in my veins it was it lessened the pain throbbing in my ankle.

I took three steps and I suddenly didn't know if the stairs were above my head or below my feet. My heel slipped on the worn edge of the step and I tumbled down. I couldn't surrender so easily.

Standing again, I spread out my arms and touched the cool stone walls. As long as I kept steady, I could keep on the path.

I traveled down several more flights, and with each the drug's power lessened. My head became clearer. My ankle flexed without pain. I thanked God for sparing me. I had gone years without prayer, and now I clung to every word as if I was five years old again.

Reaching the grove of silver trees I saw the princesses' colorful gowns disappearing ahead. I slowed my pace and turned my attention to the forest of silver. If this didn't convince the king of this place's existence, nothing would.

I ran my hand over the smooth bark, feeling for the weakest point. A delicate shimmer and then a snap echoed out. I plunged the branch into my satchel.

I did the same with the gold.

The diamond branches proved more difficult. I waited until I saw the women's skirts trailing far ahead. The jewels jingled prettily as I gripped the twigs, though the sharp points tore into my skin. Each was as hard as the other. I twisted, cursed, and bent the little devils every way. I contemplated stabbing the king with the shimmering twigs, asking if that were proof enough.

I looked towards the princesses. They were almost out of sight. Time was running out. I gripped the thinnest twig between both hands and in a swift movement pressed down.

It cracked through, the snap deep and piercing. Diamonds fell like hail to the ground.

Dammit.

I froze, as did Octavia and her sisters. They turned around slowly.

"Who is there?" Caroline asked of the wilderness.

I forced my breaths to remain shallow.

"There's no one," Amelia said. "Daltry was out cold. I saw him drink the wine myself. The goblet was empty."

They must have suspected me to make sure I drank it this time. Octavia didn't seem so certain. Her gaze narrowed and she approached the glittering tree I stood beside. She appeared even statelier surrounded by such beauty. Her red gown fanned out behind her like flames against snow.

She was mere inches away as she looked through my invisible form. I could smell the rose oil radiate from her skin. I could feel her breath.

I took a silent step backwards. The branches chimed delicately. Her eyes looked up at the tree, right at the gnarled edge where I had snapped the branch through.

I almost swore I saw the faintest smile pull on her pink lips.

"Let's keep going," she said. "It was nothing."

THIS NIGHT the melody infected me utterly.

I hated admitting I was sad to never see this place again. My blood tingled with youthful vigor. The misery I grew to accept lifted, and I could believe myself whole. Complete. Anxiety did not tear my soul. Doubt dared not enter my consciousness. There was only the present and the past was not even a memory.

The violins sang in my blood, and I couldn't peel my eyes

away from the pointed silk shoes spinning across the polished floor. The men's backs were beautifully arched in their tight coats, their hands perfectly positioned around the princesses' waists. They fell away with the melody, and I wanted to join them.

I grew bold.

I abandoned the edge of the ballroom where the other men waited like patient dogs. I wove between the jungle of dancing couples, entranced by the colors and sounds. Aurelia slipped past. Henrietta and her prince swayed to my left. Octavia twirled in the center. Her usual vivaciousness returned and shined through her every bend and turn.

She leaned into the grasp of her prince, her feet gliding effortlessly between his black leather boots. His fine jaw and pointed cheeks showed a man descended from a line of the bluest blood. He was everything a prince should be. I wanted to be him. I wanted to slide my hand behind her delicate waist and lead her across the gleaming floor.

A sharp pain pressed down across my foot. Something pushed hard into my shoulder. Sophia fell into a pile of skirts, my own cloak tumbling out of my anxious fingers with her.

The music stopped. The dancers came to a standstill. All eyes were on me.

I was exposed.

I only had seconds to react. I grabbed hold of a silver dinner knife off of a nearby table and held it out.

"Don't move," I warned. The blade gleamed steady.

Octavia untangled herself from the prince's grasp and took two steps towards me.

"There is no need to fear," she said, her words almost suppressing a relieved lilt.

I kept my knife pointed and ready for attack.

"Keep dancing," she commanded of the others. "Mr. Daltry is surprised, that is all."

The dark melody started again and the floor rumbled as heeled shoes struck the ground. She grabbed hold of my hand and peeled my fingers back, allowing the knife to clang at our feet.

"Come," she said.

I had no choice but to listen. She led me down a white hallway into a room of blue silk and gold filigrees. Candles burned in golden candelabras, their dim light illuminated by mirrors hanging on every wall. She approached a carved wooden table and poured us each a glass of wine.

She handed it to me, and I peered distastefully at the dark liquid. She chuckled.

"Don't worry," she said, sitting on a cream damask settee. "This one isn't a sleeping draught."

She held hers up to her lips and took a sip. I followed suit, not yet wanting to speak. There were many things to say, and yet I couldn't think of a single one.

Silence separated us.

"Are you going to tell Father?" she asked, breaking the growing tension.

I took another sip of the wine. Understanding filled her eyes.

"You already have," she said. "Yet, we are still down here. He didn't believe you, did he?"

"No," I pushed out.

She put her glass down on the gilded table beside her.

"Father always was short sighted," she said, drumming her fingers on her gown. They looked so white compared to the deep red of the silk. "He won't believe anything unless he has proof."

I rummaged through my bag and pulled out the diamond twig. The jewels glinted and sparkled in the candlelight. Octavia rose from the settee and approached me, her blonde curls framing her face like an aura.

"What can I offer you not to show father?" she asked.

Her eyes were locked on the little sparkling jeweled twig. She reached her hand towards the branch as if trying to snatch it away. I retracted it just out of her reach, and lunged it deep within my satchel.

"You can offer me nothing," I said. "I will not abandon the people as I was abandoned. My word was given and it cannot be broken."

I wasn't sure if my words hurt her or myself more. I turned and aimed for the door, but I stopped when a firm hand gripped my wrist.

"Please," she pleaded. "You spoke to me of an escape. How if you wander, you never have to think on your misfortunes. This place. This dance. This is our escape. Without it, we are nothing but prisoners."

I tore my wrist out of her grasp and faced her.

"Your misfortunes?" I asked, fuming. "You speak as if a child. What do you have to escape from? Riches? Food? What a prison you have. I'm sure every peasant starving in the gutter would be understanding of your plight."

Her features sharpened.

"It is a prison!" she cried back. "Every night we are locked in. Our every move is watched and critiqued. Our fates are written on paper and traded to the highest bidder. Is that not the definition of a prisoner?"

I remained silent. Indignant.

"We are cargo, Mr. Daltry. As women we have no rights. All we have is our charm and a pretty face," she spat. "Everyone believes we lead a blessed life, but the crown comes before all else."

"You are much too dramatic."

"Were you not offered one of us?"

Something flashed within her eyes, something like anger or resentment. As quickly as I saw it, it disappeared and I was left with a lingering chill. She circled me, trailing her slender finger across my shoulder and down my back. My eyes closed despite myself.

"I believe that is part of the deal if you discover our secret. You get to choose the daughter that pleases you most," she let her hand slide down my chest. She smiled as if enjoying seeing the pleasure rippling over me. "The one that grows the desire you now try to hide from me, Mr. Daltry."

I felt the heated pressure coiled between my thighs. I cursed my weakness. She grabbed my jacket and pulled me against her. Her lips grazed past my ears and my heart pounded.

"Damn be her choice if she wants you," she whispered.

She released my coat and pushed me back. Calm smoothed her features.

"I never thought..." my throat was dry.

"Men usually don't," she said. "As children my sisters and I realized our fates rested in the hands of the bearded men surrounding father. We knew we would be separated. All we could do was pray. And we did. Fevered prayers never to be parted."

"What came of these prayers?" I asked, straightening my jacket.

"A fairy godmother answered," she replied. "She gave us a gift. A secret. No matter where we would be, we could always come here and be together as sisters. This is the only place we can be free. Escape all that palace nonsense and be ourselves for a few hours. However, she gave us a warning. If the secret of the dance is ever told and believed, it will vanish."

Pleading filled her sad eyes. They were lost and I thought I looked into my own reflection. When you have no choice but darkness before you. My heart quaked for her, and in that moment I knew she was right. We were both prisoners to the crown.

"You have already told our secret," she whispered, tears threatening behind her words. "But please don't make father believe with your proof."

She reached for my hand and pulled me to her. I slid my arm behind her waist and the other one into her hair. She cupped my cheeks and skated her fingernails behind my ears and down my neck. Her sweet breath was hot and the scent of rose overwhelming. She tilted her chin towards me and I claimed her plump lips with my own.

Warmth rushed over and through me. I was bewitched. I would give her anything...

I pushed her away. Her eyes searched me as if wondering what was the matter. I would give her anything, except what she asked.

"You are asking me to commit treason, not just against the king, but my own heart," I said, placing her hands down at her sides. "I gave my word to the people. Your father expects an answer, one I am determined to give. There is nothing more to be done. My word is unbreakable, even if I wish to break it."

Red blossomed across her face and within her eyes. Through the red mist infecting her expression, I swear I saw an odd flicker of relief. She turned away, and I saw only her back.

"That's it then?" she asked, sitting back on the settee.

"There is no other recourse," I replied. "The first night I saw with my eyes this place, it was over. There was no going back."

I knelt next to her. She still faced away from me, her delicate hands coiled in her lap. I wanted to take one and stroke it until she forgave me, but I resisted. It would only make everything harder.

"If the secret is ever told and believed, it will all vanish," she whispered, as if she were speaking to a ghost.

She breathed deeply and her gaze snapped back to me. I was surprised there was no more anger or sadness.

"I cannot stay cross at you," she said. "You are a man of honor and only following what you naturally are."

I ground my teeth, the word "honor" stinging my heart.

"It's always been my strength, but now it is almost a curse," I said.

"Everything is as it must be," she said. "Life will continue, though I will miss the dance."

I never hated myself more in any moment of my life. I was weak and helpless. Except...

"What if I waited to tell the king?" I asked.

Her eyes brightened and a coy smile spread on her lips.

"What do you mean?" she asked.

"Your father gave me three days and three nights to figure out your secret. I do not have to tell him tomorrow. I can at least give you one more night," I said.

She wrapped her arms around my neck and squeezed. She kissed my cheek.

"You are a prince, even though you do not realize it."

CHAPTER 7

I couldn't stop staring at the three branches of silver, gold, and diamonds. I couldn't stop hearing her voice.

If the secret of this place is ever told and believed, it will vanish

The twigs were enchantingly beautiful, and I was about to cause them to disintegrate into nothing.

The last thing I thought I would ever feel was pity for a princess, yet here I was, sulking over three pretty branches. I used to know who I was and how I felt. I hated anyone who claimed their blood made them able to rule other men. I hated God for forsaking me. Now, I clung to the small crucifix like a frightened child.

Unable to bear it anymore, myself anymore, I tucked the branches safely away in my satchel. Tomorrow I would still go before the king and he would know the truth. Be damned if I stopped now. But my determination couldn't erase my guilt. I had to see her.

The pain in my ankle returned and prickled and snapped with every step.

I caught Octavia's smooth voice coming from the salon.

The door was cracked, and I peered in. Charlotte and Sophia stood before their sister surrounded by deep yellow silk walls.

"Are you sure about Daltry?" Charlotte asked, sitting on a velvet chair. "He is so different from all the others."

"That is the point," Octavia said.

"He has been quite surprising," Sophia added.

She sat beside her sister. Octavia remained standing, her arms crossed.

"You are certain he is determined to present his proof to father?" Charlotte asked.

She lifted the crystal lid of a small bowl and picked out a small biscuit. She pushed the treat into her mouth and let out a satisfied sound.

"Quite certain," Octavia said, almost with a hint of triumph. "He is a man of his word, Charlotte. Him refusing me proves it."

"We must make sure tonight is a true celebration then," Sophia said, clapping her hands.

I refused to be an eavesdropper any longer. I coughed and opened the door. They spun up from their seats and curtsied, their muslin skirts delicate and sheer.

"Mr. Daltry," they said in unison.

"Might I have a word alone with Octavia?" I asked, trying to not trip over my own words.

They nodded their heads, although Charlotte took one more biscuit from the crystal bowl before they left.

Octavia strolled to a velvet chair beside a marble fireplace and sat down. She leaned forward and straightened her blue silk sash around her waist.

"What could cause you to search me out, Mr. Daltry?" she asked.

I lurched towards her, the vibrant Persian rug muffling the clicks of my cane.

"I know I cannot take away your burdens," I said. "But…"

"Mr. Daltry, please," she interrupted with all kindness. "We are passed that."

I dug into my pocket and pulled out the small silver crucifix. It dangled on its chain. She looked at it, then at me with confusion.

"I've had this longer than I can remember," I said. "For a time I believed it a joke, but it has provided me with strength. I want to give it to you."

I stretched it out to her, the little figure swinging side to side. She stared as if not knowing what to do. Her mouth fell slack.

"There is no need for tokens," she said, leaning slightly back in her chair.

"Please," I said. I grabbed her hand and placed it inside. "It will give me comfort knowing you have it regardless."

I released her and she examined the dead figure with a look of amusement. She stood and stepped towards me. She stroked my cheek and gazed into my eyes. I thought they would be riddled with sadness, but instead her blue eyes were nothing but calm waters. I hoped my gift had already settled her torment.

"Your soul is heavy," she cooed. "Don't let it be. You are an exceptional man. Brave, strong, and true. Countless men have died unable to achieve such character. Don't be one of them."

Brave, strong, and true, the Oracle's voice echoed.

She smiled sweetly and her hand slid off my cheek. She curtsied, still holding tightly to the crucifix. Nearing the door, she pressed the little golden handle and left.

"Until tonight, Mr. Daltry."

THERE WAS no false pretense this final night. They dressed openly before me, twirling in their gowns of silk and shoes of satin. I leaned back in my embroidered chair, not knowing what else to do and closed my eyes. I could still see them dance in the darkness. The melody swirled around me like a ghost refusing to be vanquished. I wished I could hear it once more.

"Mr. Daltry," Matilda's voice jarred me. "Octavia requests you accompany us tonight."

My eyes flashed open and I saw Matilda and Aurelia standing before me. Their features seemed lifted, as if illuminated with some happy knowledge.

"Accompany?" I asked.

They nodded their heads, curls bouncing every which way.

"Octavia wants you to be her prince tonight," Aurelia said. Her gaze glistened with a dark eagerness.

"She can't be serious," I protested. "I am the reason you will never return to your secret kingdom."

"All will be as it should, Mr. Daltry," Matilda encouraged.

They both extended their hands out to me. I leaned on my cane and stood. Aurelia's lips puckered in sour disappointment. Matilda clucked her pink tongue.

"You won't be needing that silly thing," Aurelia said. She slid her arm beneath mine as Matilda snatched my cane away and leaned it against the chair. I didn't like being without it, but they seemed unconcerned.

"How do you expect me to walk?" I asked.

Matilda took my other arm and gave it a small squeeze.

"We will be your support tonight. Besides, once we get down to below, you won't feel any more pain and will have little use of a cane," Matilda said.

"It would be quite useless," Aurelia giggled.

They led me to their chamber, their silk gowns sweeping the smooth wooden floorboards. The other princesses stood as if waiting for me, large smiles on their prim faces. Charlotte held a man's jacket of deep red. Dorothea a pair of folded down black leather boots. Before I could say a word, Caroline grabbed hold of my collar and peeled it down my back and off my arms. Charlotte directed my hands to slide into the new vibrant coat.

"What's all this?" I asked.

They laughed at me as Sophia wrapped a piece of long, white cotton around my neck until it touched the base of my chin.

"If you are to be a prince, then we must make you as presentable as a prince," Camilla said. She unraveled the simple black bow around my hair and retied it with one made of silk.

"Who are these other princes?" I asked.

"They are from many different kingdoms," Caroline said, as if it were quite plain.

Henrietta straightened my jacket and smoothed the wrinkles that puckered the luxurious fabric.

"Don't worry about them," Camilla said. "You are their equal in every way."

My desire for further questions ceased when Octavia appeared from behind a screen. She was dressed in a stunning gown of black that sparkled like the night sky. Her blonde curls were tight and lightly powdered, except for the waterfall of yellow flowing down her back. In her perfect hands she held a perfect band of gold.

A crown.

Her red painted lips smiled as she lifted it high above me and placed it on my head.

"I crown you Prince Ross Daltry," she said. She let her hands graze down my arms until clasping my hands firmly within hers. "Now that you are a proper prince, you may be my escort."

I was speechless. She should have hated me, they all

should, and yet they were showing me every kindness. I felt an utter fraud. I wanted to remove myself from her touch, but she quickly wrapped her arm behind my elbow. Amelia took the other and I was surprised by their strength.

"I told you, Mr. Daltry," Octavia said. "You must show no guilt. You have behaved as a prince and are to be rewarded as a prince."

The four poster bed and the navy canopy started to tremble. The gears ground beneath our feet and the chains rattled in piercing notes. The bed sunk and the doorway opened, revealing the spiral staircase leading towards heaven.

I WAS A STRONG YOUTH AGAIN. A man capable with a bright future ahead of him. Down the spiral staircase we flew, past the grove of silver and gold, through the forest of diamonds until we stopped at the lake's edge. As all the times before the princes in the rowboats cut through the gloom, except with one small difference. One of the boats was empty.

"It is customary the prince help the princess into the boat," Octavia said as the vacant boat tore through the sandy shore.

I nodded, and happily glided my hands around her waist and lifted her as if she weighed as much as a sparrow into the boat. Leaping in myself, I grabbed the oars and sliced through the black water towards the illuminated castle.

The thin strings of the violin vibrated my soul. The plucks of the harpsichord my blood. Octavia's eyes deepened and glittered as black as the water surrounding us. She appeared triumphant, and I wanted to please her always.

Entering the castle the princes lead the princesses to the polished dance floor of inlaid wood. Immediately they swayed with the rhythm of the dance, their vibrant skirts entangling between the thick leather boots of their stately escorts.

Octavia squeezed my arm.

"Shall we join?" she asked.

Fear gripped my throat at the swirling colors and sea of smiling faces.

"I hardly know how anymore," I said.

She raised her perfectly shaped eyebrows and shook her head as if I had told an amusing joke.

Taking my wrist she placed my hand behind her waist. She laid her right hand on my shoulder and pulled me tight against her. With every breath I took her bosom pressed into my chest. Our fingers entwined and I could feel her heart beating in the valleys of her hot palms.

"Fall away with me," she whispered in my ear.

The music could finally consume me. Sound rushed over and through me as she pulled me across the polished floor. My legs slipped between hers as we spun and circled, the feel of her body wrapping me in warm velvet. Growing bold, I pressed her closer, reveling the sensation of her breasts and hips pressing against me. Her flesh burned beneath her silk bodice, and I wondered how much hotter she would feel naked.

We danced entranced by the melody I know not how long. I never once looked upon the ancient grandfather clock. Time stopped except for our shoes. The thick leather of my boots split, and I saw a ruby fly off of Octavia's shoe, but still we continued. I didn't want to stop. If I stopped it would be over, and reality would reign over us once more.

Shreds of satin whispered across the wooden floor. Pearls skated beneath our feet. A chorus of falling jewels and cracking heels echoed out like a summer storm.

She squeezed my hand and I pulled her even tighter against me. I wanted her heat. I wanted her.

Slowing, I lifted her powdered chin and brought her lips up to mine and kissed her deeply. Longingly, as if I would never kiss another woman in all my days. Her hands slid up my back and her fingers coiled in my hair. Fire burned in their wake.

She pulled away, leaving my pounding lips hungering to taste her again. Her eyes smoldered with a black desire and she tugged on my jacket leading me away from the couples that continued to dance.

We ran down a dim hall populated by marble statues of women frozen in dominating positions. I imagined her as such a woman. Strong and unafraid. She stopped before a door edged in gold and embraced me in a kiss once more. I fumbled for the latch and clicked it open. We staggered inside, our eyes closed and mouths roving insatiably over one another.

Her hot fingers slid my jacket off my shoulders and tore through my cravat. I hiked up her black skirts and filled my hands with her smooth buttocks. She licked my ear and left a trail of wet kisses down my now exposed neck and tore open my shirt. She pushed me back and I obeyed, falling into a cushioned chair. Lifting her gown up to her waist she straddled my hips and rocked into me. I hissed in pleasure before she took my lips again. Her hot tongue danced over my teeth and I grabbed her hips pressing them harder against my growing desire.

A click echoed out through our moans. Something hard and cold locked around my left wrist.

She grabbed my arm and swung it behind, the right imprisoned as the left. I tried to pull them free, but I couldn't. A wicked sort of satisfaction glimmered across her features.

"What is the meaning of this?" I asked, confusion sweeping over me.

The bonds rattled as I continued to struggle. She placed her finger over my lips.

"There is nothing to fear," she said. "You are only getting the reward you deserve."

There was an edge to her town that sent a chill down my spine. I rocked in the chair, trying to throw myself to the floor in an effort for escape, but she only laughed at me.

"Let me out of these infernal bonds," I demanded.

"Why should I do that?" she asked. "You would never stay still otherwise and trust me, you will need to stay still."

She rose from my lap and sauntered to a gilded table of red and gold. She gripped something off the surface, and it was only when she faced me again I saw what it was. A silver blade flashed in her hand, and she gave a happy chuckle as she ran her finger down the length. Fear struck my core, cold and consuming.

"You are nothing but a murderer!" I seethed. "You are going to kill me so I don't tell your precious secret."

She clucked her tongue and pulled out a small strap of leather. She scraped the edge of the blade up and down in solid strokes.

"Those are harsh words of which you know nothing about," she said. "I've never killed a soul unlike my wretched father. I've only ever offered salvation to those worthy enough."

"You lie," I spat. "This has all been a ruse and I was a fool taking the bait."

I tried to pull my wrists free, but I cried out as tendons snapped and metal tore into my skin. She rushed to me, concern in her eyes.

"Don't do that," she said. "I know it is not your nature to accept defeat, but I assure you it's quite useless. There is no need to cause yourself further harm."

I ground my teeth together and took several hard breaths.

Once she was satisfied I would not attempt breaking my own hands and wrists again, she returned to sharpening her knife blade.

"You want me to be perfect for when you filet me?" I asked. "To think I thought you needed saving."

Her eyes flashed red. She walked in quick and determined steps to me and pointed the knife point right at my nose.

"That is the only thing that disappoints me in you," she said, running the blade softly down the side of my nose and across my cheek. She let it rest on my lips now. "I and my sisters are quite capable of saving ourselves. Just because we lack the physique of a man doesn't make us less capable."

She scraped the blade every so gently off of my lip, leaving a biting sting. She returned to the table and put away the strap of leather and laid the knife down on a pillow of velvet.

"I can't fault you for such a belief, Ross," she said, pulling out the crucifix I had given her. It dangled mocking my entrapment. "That is the natural flaw inherent in all men. They think they are our great protectors, when really they are the reason for our suffering."

Holding it between her fingers she snapped it in two and threw it across the room.

"Is that why you seek to punish us?" I growled.

Surprise washed over her expression.

"Never punish!" she exclaimed. "We only seek out those men who have attained a certain nobility about their person. Men like you, Ross. I wanted you since I first saw you. So gruff. Mysterious. A thick layer of hardened crust of which beneath laid a heart of gold. You did have me worried once or twice, but you succeeded each time."

My heart stilled and cold sweat trickled down my temples. A horror I never experienced gripped me and I knew it wanted to crush me.

"What madness are you speaking of?"

"Men always have to be shown," she lamented.

She clapped her hands in three thunderous strikes. The doors flung open and in entered her other sisters. They were now shrouded in delicate fabrics of gray from head to foot, their faces covered by a sheer veil. They appeared as a religious order of ghosts or witches.

What struck me more were the princes they danced with every night standing beside them. Their eyes were blank and features unmoving. The princesses grabbed them by the shoulders, spun them around and pushed them down to their knees. The men kissed the hems of the princess's dresses and the white tips of their fingers.

Octavia approached a prince with black hair that skimmed his shoulders. He turned to her and kissed her pointed shoe. She snapped her fingers and he kneeled before her, back tall and straight. She unraveled his cravat until his neck was bare. A thin scar ran from the top of his neck to the base. The other sisters demanded their princes do the same. They untangled their cravats from their skin all revealing the same, thin scar.

"They are your slaves," I said. I couldn't tell if my heart beat rapidly or not at all anymore.

They laughed in a chorus.

"They are not slaves," Octavia corrected. "They are chosen."

A panic for survival struck my core. I pulled at my bonds again, trying to keep them from noticing my straining. If I could bend my thumb in slightly, I could slip one hand free. One hand was all I needed.

"I left out one part of the magic the godmother gave us," she continued. "The ability that man may never separate us. To bind to us men of a certain...caliber. For the magic to work, you have to have certain qualities. To be a worthy prince, a man must be brave, strong, and true."

Brave, strong, and true, the Oracle's voice echoed.

My God.

"When have I ever been any of those things," I spat, my hand cramping, tearing, as I tried to press it through. I swallowed down a hiss of agony as the bone finally snapped.

She took the knife again and neared me. Sweat rolled down my forehead and back. I hated her. Hated her as I should have from the beginning.

"You were brave taking father's challenge," she cooed. "You were strong fighting through the wine we made you drink. You were true when wouldn't go back on your word, even for me. This is why you will avoid the gallows. The others either succumbed to the laudanum or made it down here only to succumb to our charms."

Giggles swirled within the pain consuming my head.

"These were all the ones chosen," she said, pointing to the princes still on their knees. "They passed our tests, just as you have unwittingly done."

Her sisters began to chant the phrase, "he must be brave, strong, and true."

"Please," I begged. My entire wrist burned. Another pop of bone and sinew and I bit the inside of my cheek tasting blood. "Show mercy."

"He must be brave, strong, and true."

"I am showing you mercy," she said. "I am taking away your pain. I am giving you the woman you desire most. That is what you want, isn't it?"

I tore at my bonds with all my strength. My hand was almost through, my broken thumb starting to glide beneath the metal.

"Hush, Ross...it's as it must be," she said. "Now stay very still, or else I might miss."

She straddled me again, her legs pressing into my hips.

"Flesh of my flesh and bone of my bone," she said. Her sisters chanted the same.

I felt my hand slide free when searing pain cut through the side of my neck. Their voices were internal now. Encompassing. I was unable to move anymore, as if an invisible force froze me.

I could only watch in silent horror as Octavia touched the blistering wound and whispered in a strange language. She lifted her fingers to her mouth, and they dripped with my blood. She licked them one at a time as if savoring a fine Chianti. Smiling gleefully with blood stained lips she pricked the tip of her thumb, watching in fascination as a red bead rose to the surface.

She dove her thumb in-between my lips, and it was her blood that now invaded my mouth. I tried to spit it out, but as the hot metallic lingered on my tongue, the hatred I had for her faded. Her cheeks grew rosier than I remembered. Her lips more red. She was a goddess. How had I not seen it before?

She removed the simple band of gold from my hair and tossed it aside. Sophia brought her a larger one on a pillow.

How thoughtful and kind of Sophia.

Octavia lifted it from its cushion and placed it on my head. I wanted to fall on my knees to her for granting me such a gift.

"My princess," I said.

"My prince," she replied. "Now and forever."

CHAPTER 8

Prince Crispin of Greybrook

"You will have three days and three nights to solve the mystery of the shoes," King Rupert said. "If you do not succeed, death awaits you."

"I have no fear," I said.

Worry pulled on his lips and his eyes grew vacant, as if seeing a ghostly mist. He caught himself, and cleared his throat.

"Our previous challenger had the same sentiment," he said, his voice rough with anger. "Yet, he wasn't even brave enough to face the gallows. What a soldier he proved to be. Ran off once he realized he would fail. I trust you will face your fate as the brave prince I know your father, King Theodore, raised?"

What a fool that soldier was. The coward. What threat could a group of harmless women possibly pose, besides boring one with talk of lace and stockings?

"Of course, Sire," I said.

"I am happy to have a born prince be our new challenger,"

he said. "If you can win this challenge you will be my sole heir and can marry whichever daughter you please. Octavia was to be wed to a king in Denmark, but he had the indecency to die."

He turned to one of the guards and nodded. The guard left, only to quickly return.

The tapping of heeled shoes and shifting of fabric echoed down the hall. The servant returned and held the door open as a throng of young women walked in. Tight curls sprung out around pretty faces before cascading past their slender shoulders.

They lined up before their father and gave a deep curtsy.

"My daughters," King Rupert said, looking upon them with fatherly pride. "The youngest Aloysia, then we have Caroline, Dorothea, Charlotte, Camilla, Aurelia, Henrietta, Sophia, Amelia, Matilda, and the eldest, Octavia. Ladies, this is Prince Crispin of Greybrook. Our newest champion."

"Pleasure to meet you, Prince Crispin," they all said in unison.

They were all uncommonly beautiful, but I could not pull my gaze away from Aurelia. Her face was a becoming mixture of soft arcs and slender points. But it was her delectable smile that entranced me the most. Supple lips the shade of peach.

For two seconds, I wanted to feel her lips against my own.

Laila

After my mother's death, I was at the complete mercy of my father. To put it plainly, he was a drunk, spending what little money our small mill earned on liquor and women instead of food for his family. Forgetting his own pain came at the cost of his child, and I often believed my mother was lucky the plague took her when it did.

Father had another vice that caused me greater fear than being turned out on the streets. He loved to boast, and my heart was crowded with humiliation and anger because of it.

I hated the jackals he attracted to our doors from this dangerous pastime. He would tell of great adventures he never took, discoveries he never made, and of his singular daughter, who possessed talents she never had. It made me ill imagining how he drank in the impressed gazes of the crowd, as his tapestry of lies grew ever thicker.

Now I was one and twenty and working as hard as any man trying to escape the threat of ruin. All I had was the prospect of a fortuitous marriage, but who would have me in this state? Not even Ernis, the fishmonger's son, wanted to make me an offer anymore.

I dragged a full sack of flour across the dirt floor and threw it with the others. The fire behind me snapped and spit, and I ducked just in time to miss the low beams of our sinking home. The walls leaned to the right, and when the wind blew the entire building moaned.

Shaking off the layer of flour from my skin, I looked back at the orders still waiting to be filled. Eight bags, each promising the coins we so desperately needed to survive. My fingers ached, but rest was a luxury I couldn't afford.

Besides, the pain distracted me from thinking of my father's ramblings at the pub. Last year, one of his tales nearly got us arrested. He claimed he killed a king's deer, and that I cooked it into a stew more delicious than the crown's own cook's. Thankfully, I was able to prove our innocence and the gallows were averted. This time.

Moments like that made my black thoughts boil and seethe, though I hated to admit to them. My life was a never-ending series of nightmares thanks to that man. Resentment festered, and in the deepest part of my heart, I secretly wished death would take him, for my sake, but also for his. Maybe then, he would finally be free from his pain.

I was just tying the sack closed when I heard footsteps approaching outside. It was early morning by now, just in time for my father to come home from the pub and sleep off the whiskey. If I were lucky, he would be too drunk to tell me of his conquests...or his lies.

Gravel and dirt crunched beneath his feet in a nerve-wracking rhythm. But as they drew closer, the sound grew into a terrifying, muffled chorus of footsteps, jangling metal, and indistinct shouts.

I dropped the sack and opened the door to see four

guards marching towards our mill, a mule following behind them. The mule dragged a small prison wagon, my father its rope-bound cargo. My cheeks flushed with anger and fear.

A rough hand pushed me out of the way as the guards filled the room, the pungent smell of beer, dirt, and horses wafting around them.

"Father! What have you done?" I asked hotly as they dragged him inside, his face ashen as he blubbered nonsense about spinning wheels and gold.

I was stopped by the outstretched arm of a particularly grisly-looking guard with a mesh of scars stretching like a net across his face. An insignia of a lion roaring on his breastplate told me he was not just a simple guard, but their captain.

"This the girl?" the captain demanded of my father, a sneer stretching the scars into a gruesome map as he turned to me. He grabbed my hands and examined them closely.

"I told them! I told them about your spinning, Laila!" Father whimpered. "But they wouldn't believe your gifts otherwise. I couldn't have them thinking I produced a talentless daughter. I had no choice but to protect my honor."

"You fool!" I cried. Horror rushed like cold water over every muscle of my body. "What have you told them this time? What lies have you spewed out of that foul mouth of yours?"

He only quivered like a common street rat and for the first time in his life was silent. I was on my own to save our lives, just as before with the deer.

"Your presence is required immediately before the king," the captain's voice cut in. "Your father finally revealed the secret you've been keeping hidden from his majesty. You're both lucky if you don't lose your heads for concealing such an extraordinary gift. If you can do half of what we heard, the king is in for quite the surprise."

"I don't have any secrets," I seethed, standing before the

captain. "Whatever he has told you is a delusion. A bit of whiskey and a great deal of madness."

His eyes narrowed and he pointed a callused finger at me.

"That is for the king to decide," he hissed back. "You might be playing the fool with me, but I wouldn't try that little game with his majesty if I were you."

"I would not dare jest about something like this," I pleaded. "Don't you realize my father is out of his mind? Look at him! Look around you. Count the leaks coming in through the roof! We have nothing. Can't you see?"

"Do you really want to know what I see?" the captain snapped. "What I see are either two peasants keeping a secret and preventing the king from what he is owed, or two liars that deserve to be hanged for treason."

His breath stank of ale. Rage ate at me that he insisted on believing my drunken father's drunken lies. Fear made me bold.

"I demand you tell me what secret I am accused of keeping," I stated coldly. "What treason have I committed?"

"*She demands*," another guard mocked. Laughter erupted all around, its dark, full sound making me feel small—worse, weak and helpless. "For someone who can spin straw into gold, you'd expect she'd be a bit more refined in her manner of speaking."

The sensation of fire seared my lungs and charred my hope as everything became clear.

"Is that truly what this is all about?" I wheezed, pushing the words through my tightening throat. "You think I can spin straw into gold? Surely you know that's not possible! It's only the ravings of a drunk! Father, tell them the truth. Tell them it was only the drink!"

My father gazed glassily at me, his lips stubbornly slack. Every second of silence that followed might as well have been a knife in my back.

The captain laughed deep from his lungs as he patted my father on the shoulder.

"Good lad. For once your father knows when to keep silent," he said. "You, on the other hand, could learn a lesson from him. I have dogs that are trained better than you."

I couldn't control my temper any longer. Before I realized what foolishness I was doing my hand flew out towards his face, but his hand gripped my wrist, stilling my attack. My head snapped back as strong fingers grabbed my hair. The cold bite of a dagger pressed against my neck as the captain seethed.

"Such violence is not becoming of a woman, although it is hard to tell if you even are a woman under such a layer of filth." His men roared with laughter. "I've had enough of your theater. If you say one more word, I swear I will cut out your tongue! You don't need to talk to spin gold for the king. Follow your father's example. I told him if he remained quiet he might stand a chance of survival, and so far he is thriving."

I knew it was useless, even treasonous to fight. Yet, I couldn't help struggling against his grip as he bound my hands with rope. My legs flailed and jerked as I kicked out. I spit in their faces as I tried to pull away again, but their grips only tightened.

I struck one's face with my foot with a resounding, satisfying crack, and his nose spurted blood.

"Make her still!" he exclaimed, wiping the crimson away with his dirty hand.

Pain sliced through my skull like lightning as something hard hit the back of my head. Everything blurred into smears of colors. My legs gave way and I fell to the ground limp and defeated.

"Merick, take her to the prison wagon," a voice ordered as they dragged me outdoors.

My father's voice echoed somewhere in the distance

begging for forgiveness. I saw the lightening sky through black bars and hard wood pressed into my back.

Everything spun, and darkness ate up my incoherent world.

~

FIND *SPIN: A Fairy Tale Retelling (Spindlewind Trilogy Book One)* at a wide selection of online retailers!

THANK YOU!

I sincerely hope you enjoyed reading this book as much as I enjoyed writing it. If you did, I would greatly appreciate a short review on Amazon or your favorite book website, such as Goodreads! Reviews are crucial for any author, and even just a line or two can make a huge difference.

NOVELS

The ***Spindlewind Trilogy***, a dark fantasy, paranormal romance retelling of Rumpelstiltskin

Spin

Twist

Break

❧

NOVELLAS

Crimp

A gothic romance. Enjoy as a stand alone work, or as a companion to the *Spindlewind Trilogy*.

ABOUT THE AUTHOR

Genevieve Raas is an international bestselling author living in the US with her husband and rather haughty Chihuahua, Mr. Darcy. When she isn't writing dark fairytales or fantasy, you can find her plotting out her next travel destination.

A graduate from Indiana University, Genevieve holds a Master's Degree in English and a Master's Certificate in Professional Editing. She has worked as Lead Transcriber on several published anthologies, including: The Collected Stories of Ray Bradbury, Volume 2 and the New Ray Bradbury Review.

Now, she is venturing out on her own, into the wilds of untamed lands and untold stories.

Genevieve loves connecting with her readers!
www.genevieveraas.com
genevieveraas@genevieveraas.com

9 781944 912185